#7

TAKE YOUR BASE

DEAN HUGHES

ALADDIN PAPERBACKS

First Aladdin Paperbacks edition August 1999

Copyright © 1999 by Dean Hughes

Aladdin Paperbacks
An imprint of Simon & Schuster
Children's Publishing Division
1230 Avenue of the Americas
New York, NY 10020

Also available in an Atheneum Books for Young Readers hardcover edition.

The text for this book was set in Caslon 540 Roman.

Printed and bound in the United States of America

10   9   8   7   6   5   4   3   2   1

The Library of Congress has cataloged the hardcover edition as follows:
Hughes, Dean, 1943–
Take your base / by Dean Hughes.
p. cm.—(Scrappers ; #7)
Summary: As the Scrappers continue to advance toward the summer
championship, Jeremy and his fellow players work to improve their
baseball skills.
ISBN 0-689-81930-7 (hardcover).—ISBN 0-689-81940-4 (pbk.)
[1. Baseball—Fiction.] I. Title.
II. Series: Hughes, Dean, 1943-   Scrappers; #7.
PZ8.3.H86625Tak   1999   [Fic]—dc21   99-20993

CHAPTER ONE

Jeremy Lim stood a few feet outside the batter's box and waited for the Whirlwinds' pitcher to take his final warm-up pitches. He leaned the bat against his leg, took off his batting helmet, and used his sleeve to wipe his forehead. He was already soaked with sweat.

The air over the field was still and hot, like the inside of an oven. Jeremy could hear the infielders talking. David Park, the second baseman, was saying, "Don't worry about Jeremy. He's so little, I doubt he can even . . ." Jeremy missed the rest. But he could see that Park and the shortstop, Gary Gunnarson, were looking his way and laughing.

Jeremy was instantly angry. Okay, so he was short. So what? He could play better than either one of those jerks. He was a whole lot faster, and he got on base more.

Still . . . Jeremy hated being small. It hadn't bothered him much in grade school, but now he was in junior high. All the other kids were growing and Jeremy wasn't. He was tired of looking up when he talked to girls. And he was tired of guys laughing at him.

When the umpire said, "Okay, let's play ball!" the Whirlwind infielders started their chatter. Chuck Kenny, the first baseman, shouted, "Okay, we got this guy." That was the usual thing to say. But Park yelled, "Hey, Jeremy, are you standing in a hole?" And Gunnarson yelled, "No, I think he's on his knees."

"You guys better *look out*," Jeremy muttered to himself.

He focused hard as he leaned over the plate. He wanted to smack that ball right at Park—rip his glove off. Maybe his arm.

Jeremy had been the leadoff hitter all season, but he knew part of that was because he got walked a lot. Pitchers had a hard time aiming at his small strike zone. Coach Carlton kept telling him to take advantage of that to get on base. When Jeremy did swing, he usually did what the coach had taught him: he just slapped the ball out of the infield for a single.

But he was sick of getting on base because he was short. And he was sick of hitting little bloopers in front of the outfielders. He wanted to slam a line drive somewhere, maybe even put one over the fence.

The first pitch came in high—up even with his chin—but he took a wild swing at it.

"Come on, Jeremy, pick your pitches!" Coach Carlton yelled from the third base coach's box. "Make him throw strikes."

Wanda Coates, the assistant coach, was saying the same thing. "Make him pitch to you, Jeremy."

That was all code language. It meant, "Don't swing, and you might get a walk."

Jeremy adjusted his batting helmet. It had slipped down over his eyes. He knew the coaches were right—in a way. It was stupid to swing so hard and to swing at bad pitches. But Jeremy wasn't going to go to the plate hoping for a walk from now on. That was a loser's attitude. If the pitch was in there, he was going to unload on it.

The next two pitches were also high, and he

let them go by. Now he hoped that Bailey, the pitcher, would force one into the strike zone without much on it.

But Bailey's pitch was almost in the dirt. Ball three. Jeremy wanted a big fat 3 and 1 pitch he could jump on. But Bailey threw another high one, and Jeremy had to take his base, whether he wanted to or not.

As he trotted to first base, he saw Bailey shake his head with disgust. He knew what the guy was thinking. Park said it for him. "That's all right," he yelled. "No one can pitch to Jeremy. He's got no strike zone."

Gunnarson laughed. "If he bends over about two inches, his shoulders are even with his knees."

Jeremy made up his mind to show those guys something. Maybe his legs were short, but he could motor. He was going to steal second. That would put him in scoring position for Robbie Marquez, the next Scrappers batter, and it might also shut their mouths.

But he had to be careful. The coach had talked to Jeremy about watching the pitcher and not just taking off. He had been picked off a couple of times this season. He had also been thrown out at second when he didn't get a good enough jump. Lately, the coach had been telling Jeremy not to run unless he got a steal sign.

Jeremy knew that sometimes he got too eager and didn't think before he took off. But he wanted to prove to the coach that he could be aggressive and use his head at the same time.

Bailey looked over his shoulder and squinted at Jeremy for a moment, then went into his windup. Bailey wasn't big, and he had a tendency to reach way back for his power. That made his motion slow. Jeremy knew he could steal on the guy.

The first pitch had some zip on it, but it took a dive. The catcher had to hustle to scoop it up off the plate.

Bailey was off to a bad start. If Jeremy stole a base on him, that would only rattle him all the more. It might be a smart time to go. But Coach Carlton didn't touch the letters on his shirt: the signal for a steal.

Jeremy took a good lead. Then, as Bailey looked his way, he stretched the lead another step—just daring him to make his move. But

Bailey started his slow windup, and Jeremy couldn't resist. He broke for second.

The pitch was low again, but Robbie reached down and scooped it. He hit a low line drive to right field. Jeremy had gotten a great jump. As he watched the ball settle in for a base hit, he knew he wouldn't have to stop at second. He rounded the base and then trotted in to third standing up.

But Coach Carlton didn't look pleased. He called for a time-out, and then put his arm around Jeremy's shoulder and walked him away from the third baseman. "Jeremy, did I give you the steal sign?" he asked.

"No. But this pitcher has a slow windup. I knew I could make it. I figured—"

"You let me decide, Jeremy. That's how it has to be."

Jeremy was not a kid who popped off—especially not at grown-ups. He kept his mouth shut, but what he wanted to say was, "Coach, I'm on third now. The way you wanted me to play it, I might have had to stop at second."

Instead, Jeremy said, "Okay," and he walked back to the base.

Gloria Gibbs was already standing in the

batter's box. She was giving Bailey her usual cold, hard stare. Bailey threw low again.

Jeremy bobbed and faked. He wanted to keep Bailey's attention—make him nervous.

The next pitch was down the pipe, however, and Gloria hit a screamer up the middle. The ball bounced a couple of times before the center fielder scooped it up, but by then Jeremy was across home plate and Robbie was loping into second.

The Scrappers' bench made some noise when Jeremy walked into the dugout, but the enthusiasm hardly seemed real. Jeremy knew what the players were thinking. No one really thought the Whirlwinds would be tough to beat, and now the Scrappers had already scored with no outs in the first inning. Everything was going according to plan.

But Bailey was finding his groove. He popped some good fastballs at Thurlow Coates and worked him to a 2 and 2 count. Then Thurlow got a little anxious and stretched for an outside pitch. He popped it up into short center. The Whirlwinds' center fielder jogged in and made the catch.

Wilson Love stepped up. Robbie cupped his

hands over his mouth and yelled from second, "Come on, Wil! Give 'er a whack!" Wilson took a fierce cut at the first pitch—a good fastball down in the strike zone—and missed badly.

Jeremy looked at Tracy Matlock, who was sitting next to him on the bench. "Looks like Bailey has found his stuff now," he said.

"I guess," Tracy said, but she hardly seemed to be paying attention.

Jeremy decided he might as well keep his mouth shut. Everyone always said he was quiet, but when he tried to talk to the other players, they treated him like he was a nobody. Maybe *they* thought he was a runt, too. But then, why not? If the coach didn't want him to swing his bat—or use his speed to steal—why should anyone think he was any good?

With a run in and two runners on base, the Scrappers should have been fired up, but there wasn't much noise on the bench. When Wilson flied out to left field and Trent Lubak grounded out to the shortstop, everyone just filed out of the dugout and trotted—or walked—onto the field.

Adam Pfitzer was pitching today. His warm-up pitches looked a little sluggish to Jeremy, but

Chuck Kenny, the Whirlwinds' leadoff batter, swung off stride and lifted a shallow fly ball to right center.

Jeremy took off after the ball, but Thurlow called, "Mine! Mine!" and kept charging. Then he reached up and caught the ball with one hand.

But the ball should have been Jeremy's!

Coach Carlton always said the center fielder should take control of the outfield. He was the player who decided whether the ball was his or not. But Thurlow didn't seem to trust Jeremy. He took every ball he could get to.

The next batter, Russ Jenson, hit a line drive straight at Jeremy. Jeremy had no chance to catch it on the fly, but he scooped it up cleanly on the first bounce and fired to second. The runner stopped at first.

Gloria yelled, "Good job, Jeremy. That's the kind of fly ball you have trouble with." Jeremy knew what she meant. Earlier in the season, he had tried to dive and catch a couple of hits like that, and he had let the ball get past him. It bothered him that Gloria didn't have more confidence that he had learned something since then.

Gunnarson was up. He hit a lazy fly ball right to Trent in left, who made the easy catch.

So far, the Whirlwinds had looked like they were bothered by the heat. They were moving—and swinging—at half speed. But then Adam got a little too careful with Friedman, the left fielder, and walked him on four pitches.

Now the Whirlwinds had a threat going, with two runners aboard. Jeremy heard some more life coming from their dugout.

"Come on, Scrappers," Coach Carlton was yelling. "Let's look alive out there." The chatter picked up a little, but Jeremy was worried. This game was crucial. The Scrappers were one game behind the Mustangs in the standings. That meant that they couldn't afford to lose another game. It would be a disaster if they let up and blew one against the Whirlwinds—a team they should be able to beat.

Big Moose Morton stepped up to the plate. Adam tossed a fat pitch right down the middle. Luckily, Morton swung under the ball and sent it rocketing high into the air toward center. Jeremy waited, tried to get a good measure of where the ball was going, and then dropped back a few steps.

There was nothing to it. The ball dropped right into Jeremy's glove.

And then popped out again!

As the ball fell toward the ground, Jeremy flailed at it with his bare hand and managed to swat it back into the air. He got his glove under it, but it almost squirted out again. He had to clamp down on it with both hands. Finally, though, he got control of it and held it up for the ump to see.

"Out!" the umpire shouted.

Jeremy took a long breath of relief, but he kept his head down as he trotted back to the dugout. He had made the catch but still managed to look like a klutzy little kid.

On his way through the infield, Jeremy crossed paths with Gunnarson. "Nice catch," he said, but he was grinning. Gunnarson glanced at Park, who was smiling, too. And then they both broke out laughing.

Jeremy looked away from them and kept running to the dugout. He walked to the bench without saying a word, without even looking anybody in the eye. He sat down as far away from the other players as he could, but no one seemed to notice him anyway.

CHAPTER TWO

"All right, now, let's do something," Coach Carlton yelled. "Let's get some base hits."

The players yelled the same sort of stuff, but Jeremy also heard Wilson say, "Man, it's hot out there today with all that catcher's gear on."

Tracy was up to bat. She took a pitch outside, and then she triggered on the next pitch and knocked a slow bouncer straight toward Gunnarson at short.

Gunnarson waited on the ball, didn't charge it. By the time he fielded the ball, he had to hurry. He tried to get too much power on his throw, and the ball took off on him. It flew high over Kenny's head at first base.

Kenny took off after the ball—which slammed into the wire fence along the first base line—but he had no chance to get Tracy.

She was already loping into second.

Jeremy was tempted to give Gunnarson a hard time, but that wasn't his style. Still, he enjoyed listening to Kenny chew out his own teammate. The Whirlwinds always did a lot of that.

There had been a time when the Scrappers had yelled at one another, too. But the team had come together pretty well now. Jeremy just wished that *he* had a close friend on the team.

"The Whirlwinds are trying to hand this game to us," Trent yelled. "Let's *take* it. We need to get fired up."

Gloria picked up on that, and she started yelling to Adam, who was walking to the plate. But Adam swung at the first pitch and popped it up. Bailey got out of the way and let Kenny move toward the mound to make the catch.

Ollie Allman, who was playing first base today, stepped up to bat as Jeremy walked out to the on-deck circle.

Ollie took a bad swing at an outside pitch, but he played it smarter after that. Bailey kept trying to get him to chase another pitch off the plate, but Ollie wouldn't do it. Bailey ended up walking him.

As Jeremy strode to the batter's box, he heard Coach Carlton call, "This pitcher can't find the plate right now, Jeremy. Don't make it easy on him."

Or in other words, "Don't swing. Try to get a walk."

Jeremy knew that made sense. He told himself not to swing at any bad pitches.

But then Park turned around and yelled to the outfielders, "Play in. Jeremy can't hit the ball that far."

All the outfielders moved in a few steps. That meant it would be harder to slap one in front of them.

That's not what Jeremy wanted to do anyway. He had hit some long flies before. Once, he had almost hit one over the fence. This would be a perfect time to smack a ball over the outfield and drive in two runs. And shut David Park's mouth for him!

The first pitch was a little high, but Jeremy wanted it. He almost jumped off the ground he swung so hard. He fouled the ball back into the screen.

"Jeremy, that ball was high," the coach yelled. "Lay off those."

Jeremy told himself that's what he would do, too. But he saw the left fielder take another couple of steps toward the infield. He wanted, more than anything, to paste one over the guy's head—maybe blast it clear out of the place and then trot past Kenny and Park and Gunnarson.

The next pitch was even higher, but Jeremy couldn't stop himself. He took a hard swipe at it and, this time, missed completely.

Jeremy was embarrassed. He laid off the next pitch, which was up again. But the 1 and 2 pitch was right at his belt. Jeremy took a home run swing—and got nothing but air.

Jeremy spun away, mad at himself. But then, when he heard Park yell, "Jeremy thinks he's Sammy Sosa," he did something he had never done before. He tossed his bat as hard as he could. He almost hit Robbie, who was on his way to the plate.

"Time-out!" Coach Carlton yelled. He waved Jeremy over to him.

Jeremy didn't want to hear this, but he walked to the coach.

"Jeremy, what are you doing?" Coach asked.

"That kid only threw one pitch in the strike zone. The count ought to be 3 and 1 right now."

Jeremy didn't say anything.

"Why were you swinging so hard?"

"The outfield was pulled in. I just thought . . . I don't know."

"That's not your game, Jeremy. If you're going to swing, do it with some control. That's what you're good at. You know how to punch that ball into the gaps."

"Okay," Jeremy said.

Coach slapped him on the back. "That's all right. Just remember next time."

As Jeremy walked to the dugout, he told himself the coach was right. It was stupid to swing so hard and strike out. But he also knew that if he had knocked an extra-base hit, everyone would be cheering for him right now.

Jeremy hoped that Robbie would sock one out of the park and get the runs anyway. But Robbie swung hard, too, and he hit the ball high in the air. The center fielder moved a little to his right and hauled it in. The Scrappers had missed their chance. The top of the second was over, and they still had only a 1 to 0 lead.

As Jeremy ran to the field, he knew he had to settle down and start playing his own game. The coach was right.

Park led off for the Whirlwinds in the bottom of the inning. He timed one of Adam's fastballs, and he drove the ball to left field. Thurlow or Jeremy might have been able to charge the ball and make the catch, but Trent didn't have much speed. He ran toward the ball but then threw on his brakes and took it on one bounce.

Park bluffed toward second and then retreated to first as the throw came in.

The next batter was the center fielder, a boy named Tyler Waddups. He was a decent outfielder but not much of a hitter.

Adam threw a good fastball, and Waddups took a strike. Then Adam let a curve get away from him. It hung over the plate, and Waddups *killed* it. He swatted the ball so hard to left that Trent just turned around and watched it disappear over the fence.

This guy who couldn't hit had suddenly

turned into a slugger. And, boy, did he enjoy it. He trotted around the bases like he was Mark McGwire.

Jeremy knew that if he knocked one over the fence, he wouldn't show off like that. But he couldn't help thinking how much fun it would be to do it, at least once.

For the moment, however, there was something more important to think about. Maybe it was only the second inning, and the score was only 2 to 1, but Jeremy didn't like falling behind these guys, even if it was only by one run.

All the other Scrappers seemed to be thinking the same thing. They began to yell to Adam, to one another. For the first time today, they sounded like they really meant it.

But Adam seemed shook up. He walked the eighth batter, Raymond Wing, and that brought Bailey up. If Bailey got on, the top of the order would be coming up, and the Whirlwinds would have something going again.

Bailey took a called strike and then, on the next pitch, chopped a grounder toward the left side.

Robbie and Gloria both broke for the ball. Robbie cut it off and made a tough one-handed pickup. Then he got the ball away quickly to second base. Tracy caught it, dragged her left foot across the bag for the first out, pivoted, and fired to first.

Bailey had fair speed, but he was out by a full step. It was a beautiful double play—a great thing to see.

Now the team was coming to life.

Adam was fired up. He pumped some fireballs at poor Chuck Kenny. The guy was a good hitter, but Adam put some nasty fastballs on the corners of the plate, and Kenny struck out on three pitches.

Jeremy expected the Whirlwinds to feel the heat, dry up, and blow away. But it didn't happen that way. The Scrappers did get a couple of hits in the top of the third, but they left both runners on base. And then, in spite of a Gunnarson single in the bottom of the inning, the Whirlwinds also failed to score.

When the Scrappers came up in the top of the fourth, they were feeling the pressure. They were still behind 2 to 1, so it was time to score some runs.

But Adam got caught off balance and popped out to the catcher.

This was getting frustrating. Bailey was not that great a pitcher, and the Scrappers were making him look like Randy Johnson.

Ollie had a good talk with himself. Then he stepped into the box and slammed the first pitch down the right field line, past the right fielder. If Ollie had had a little more speed, he might have turned the play into a triple. But he galloped around first and stopped at second with a double.

Jeremy was up. The tying run was in scoring position. A walk wouldn't really make that much difference. What Jeremy wanted was an RBI. But if he looped a little single into the outfield, Ollie would never score. Jeremy needed to drive one hard.

"All right now, Jeremy. Just meet the ball. You know what we talked about."

That was right. Get the runner to third with one out. Robbie and Gloria could get the run home and maybe even get a big rally going. Jeremy's job was to keep things going, get another runner on base.

"Move in," Gunnarson and Park were both yelling. "Play him shallow." And this time the outfield moved in even closer than before.

The first pitch might have been outside, but it was close, and Jeremy went after it. He didn't plan to swing hard—didn't mean to—but he took a real slash at it.

The coach yelled his usual advice, and Jeremy told himself to ease off, maybe even work for the walk. But the ball came down the middle, and he jumped at it again.

And he almost came through. He simply got around too fast on the pitch and pulled it foul, down the left field line.

A few feet farther to the right, and Jeremy would have had himself a double. He actually saw Friedman, out in left, move back a few steps. That was Jeremy's chance. Now, with two strikes, he could take an easy swing and punch the ball in front of Friedman.

That's what his brain told him. But his muscles wouldn't hear of it. The next pitch was up in his eyes, and he should have let it go by. But he thrashed at the ball and missed it clean.

He didn't throw his bat this time—didn't want that much attention. He also didn't look at the coach. He just marched back to the dugout with his head down.

"What are you doing, Jeremy?" Gloria asked him. "You never swing like that. Come on. We depend on you."

Yeah, right.

Jeremy walked to the end of the bench again. He watched as Robbie hit a hard grounder to Park at second. That did move Ollie to third, but Park made the easy stop and threw Robbie out. The Scrappers were out. Another chance lost, and the score was still 2 to 1 for the Whirlwinds.

Jeremy grabbed his glove. But as he reached the opening to the dugout, Coach Carlton stepped in front of him. "Jeremy," he said, "I'm going to put Chad in the game now."

Jeremy nodded and then walked back and sat down. It was nothing new to have a sub come in for him, but not in the fourth inning. Especially not in a close game.

This was the coach's way of saying, "Play it my way or sit down."

Jeremy hardly knew what to think. He was still mad at himself. But the coach had been awfully quick to give up on him. And none of the other players seemed worried. They ran to their positions, and no one said a word about Jeremy being left on the bench.

CHAPTER THREE

Adam was pitching well now. The Whirlwinds couldn't get anything going in the fourth and fifth innings, but the Scrappers didn't score in the fifth either. When they came to bat in the top of the sixth, Jeremy could see that the Scrappers were worried.

Jeremy thought about talking to the players, trying to fire them up. That was the only thing he could do now. But it just wasn't natural for him to make a lot of noise, so he sat by himself and didn't say much of anything.

Adam had pitched a great game, yet he was in danger of losing it. He looked determined when he walked to the plate to lead off. He waited Bailey out until he got something he could drive, and then he smashed the ball past Gunnarson for a single.

The Scrappers needed to get Adam home now. The trouble was, Ollie was coming up, and then Chad. Both were doing a lot better than they had earlier in the season, but they were still the weakest hitters in the lineup—especially with runners on base.

On the first pitch, Ollie squared off to bunt. The pitch was high, so he pulled his bat back. But Jeremy could see what the coach was thinking. He wanted to get Adam into scoring position.

But now the infield moved in. Kenny moved down the first base line, in front of the bag, and Jenson did the same at third. Maybe the coach would lift the bunt sign and let Ollie hit away.

But Ollie squared off again, and this time he fouled the ball into the dirt.

"I don't get this," Thurlow said. "With those guys crowded in, he ought to smack it down their throats."

Jeremy understood what Thurlow meant. But Ollie struck out a lot. And a strikeout would leave Adam at first. It was time to trade an out to put Adam on second, time to play for just one run.

So Ollie squared off again, and this time he got the bunt down. It was a good bunt, down the third base line, but Jenson got to it quickly. He stabbed the ball and then spun toward second. Adam was anything but a speedster, but he'd broken hard for second. Jenson might have gotten him, but he didn't take the chance. He turned and threw to first for the sure out.

So Adam was on second and Chad was up. But there was little advantage in trading an out to get Adam to third. True, he wasn't fast, and he *would* have a better chance of scoring from third, but a solid hit might bring him home from second, and a second out would take the pressure off the Whirlwind infield players.

Chad seemed to take his time heading out to the box. As he walked by, he glanced at Jeremy. His look seemed to say, "I wish you were going out there, not me."

Jeremy wished he could go back in, too. He would love to have another chance to make up for those strikeouts.

Chad's father seemed to make it to all the games—even the ones on Tuesday afternoons, like this one. At least Mr. Corrigan was controlling his voice a little better these days. "This is your chance, Chad," he yelled. "You've got to come through."

More pressure on the poor kid.

Chad got set, looked at Bailey, and then called a time-out. He stepped out of the box, swung the bat once, and then stepped back in. But this time he was crowding the plate more. Jeremy wondered what he was up to.

Everyone was yelling now, on both teams. Bailey looked nervous, too. The front of his uniform was wet, and beads of sweat were forming on his forehead.

The first two pitches were outside. Chad let them go by. "Make him pitch to you," everyone was yelling now. And Chad had to know what that meant: Take the walk. Let Robbie drive the runs in.

Bailey's next pitch didn't have much on it. The only trouble was, he had gotten it way inside this time. Chad turned away, but he didn't jump out of the box. The ball whomped him in the shoulder.

"Take your base!" the umpire shouted.

"He did that on purpose," Gloria said. "Did

you see that? He took one for the team."

Jeremy thought she was right. Chad ran to first, and he looked very pleased with himself as he took his stance. Jeremy was sure Robbie or Gloria, or both of them, would come through this time. Bailey was tired.

But the Whirlwinds' coach knew that, too. He called time-out and put Gunnarson on the mound. Gunnarson was no flamethrower, but he could get the ball over the plate.

Robbie didn't show his usual patience against Gunnarson. He swung at his first pitch and got out ahead of the ball. He sent a little grounder bouncing to Jenson at third. All Jenson had to do was field the ball and step on the bag.

Jeremy felt almost sick to think the Scrappers could blow their chance for the championship by losing to the stupid Whirlwinds. Gloria had to make something happen.

Gloria looked angry, ready for the kill, and Gunnarson must have let her look bother him. He threw the ball up and down, in and out, everywhere but over the plate. He ended up walking Gloria, and now things looked good for the Scrappers again. Thurlow was up—with the bases loaded.

All the Scrappers were standing and shouting. So were their fans. The place was going crazy.

Thurlow took a mighty swing at the first pitch and fouled it out of play. Then he started to swing and tried to stop. He accidentally fouled another one into the dirt.

Thurlow got more careful after that and worked the count to 2 and 2, but then he got the pitch he wanted and took a *perfect* cut. And missed.

He slammed the bat on the ground. The pitch had simply been too big, too easy—and probably too slow.

The Whirlwinds went crazy. They still had their 2 to 1 lead, and the Scrappers would only be up one more time.

What the Whirlwinds didn't do was extend their lead in the bottom of the sixth inning. The whole team seemed worn out, and Adam, in spite of the temperature, was still throwing hard. He blew them away, three up, three down.

So it all came down to the seventh inning. The

Scrappers had one last chance. But their best hitters had batted in the sixth.

Jeremy thought he saw the season slipping away, and he knew he had been a big part of the problem. If he had slapped one of his little singles—or walked instead of striking out—the team might be ahead right now.

Still, Wilson could tie the game with one stroke. And maybe he would. He stood outside the box and timed Gunnarson's warm-up pitches, and then he played it smart. He didn't take one of his home run swings; he merely stroked the ball, smooth and easy. And he knocked the ball into center for a single.

Trent had seen all that and tried to do the same thing. He took a pitch for a ball, got a sense of the speed, and then he took a level, easy swing . . . and caught the ball *on the nose*.

The ball shot into left center and got past Friedman and Waddups. They both hustled hard, but Friedman was the one who got to it. He turned around, took a good strong stride, and fired at the cutoff man. Wilson was lumbering around the bases, going hard, and was about to round third.

Coach Carlton saw the good throw and yelled, "Stop!"

Wilson pulled up at third, and Trent, who had rounded second, had to hold up and go back.

Two runners in scoring position and no one out. Jeremy was breathing a little easier. But the Scrappers had gotten close before. This time someone had to come through, and it was Cindy Jones, in the game for Tracy, who was coming up to bat.

No one had worked harder in batting practice than Cindy had, but she was not one of the players the Scrappers wanted up when the game was on the line. The problem was, Martin Epting was also in the game now, and he was coming up after Cindy.

Cindy took a couple of pitches, but the second one was a strike. "Keep your eye on the ball," Coach yelled. "Just stroke it."

The smart-mouthed Whirlwinds infielders were all telling her she didn't have a chance. The noise in the park was really intense.

Cindy got a good pitch, and she took a nice stroke. She hit the ball high in the air to right field. The right fielder was a sub, and no great athlete. Jeremy hoped he would foul up the play. But he dropped back a few steps, made the catch for the out, and then threw as hard as he could toward home.

Wilson had tagged up, and the coach yelled, "Go!"

It was a race. The throw was not great, but it was getting there. Wilson was running like a runaway buffalo, and Moose Morton was blocking the plate. A lot of animal flesh collided at the plate, and it all ended in a pile on the ground.

But Moose didn't have the ball.

It bounded on by him, and the tying run scored.

Trent went to third on the throw, and he bluffed a move home. But Gunnarson was covering. He grabbed the ball and held Trent at third.

Jeremy took a long breath of relief. The game was tied. The Scrappers were still alive. But this was the perfect chance to take the lead: a runner on third and only one out.

Coach Carlton called to Martin before he could head to the plate, and the two talked for a few moments. Jeremy wondered what they were talking about—what kind of trick the coach might have up his sleeve.

But the "trick" was not a trick at all. The first pitch was down the middle. Martin swung down on the ball and chopped a high-bouncing ground ball toward second base.

Park fielded the ball and looked home. But it was too late. Trent was crossing the plate. So Park threw out Martin at first, but now the Scrappers had the lead, 3 to 2.

The great thing was, Martin had bounced the ball to the right on purpose. He had given himself up to get the run home.

Ollie tried hard to keep things going. He hit a hard shot to left, but Friedman hauled it in, and the game went to the bottom of the seventh.

The Scrappers ran to the field like a pride of lions, ready for the hunt. And the Whirlwinds were clearly out of air.

Kenny tried to save the day, but he struck out. And that was it. It turned into a one-two-three inning, and the Scrappers had their win.

It was a great comeback, and the Scrappers were happy.

At least most of them were. Jeremy was glad the team had won, but he wondered whether he would be part of things in the future. Had he blown his starting position for the rest of the season?

He celebrated with the other players and then got on his bike and rode home to an empty house. His parents and his older brother were all still at work, but that didn't really matter. No one in his family was into sports, not even his big brother, so none of them would have understood even if he'd been able to explain what he was feeling.

Jeremy showered and then turned on his computer. He was hoping he might have an e-mail from his cousin Eddy in California, but he hadn't gotten a single message.

What he wished was that he had a friend on the team to talk things over with. He thought about calling Robbie, but after the way he had played today, he was too embarrassed.

CHAPTER FOUR

Jeremy was still feeling pretty rotten when he got to practice the next morning. When he saw Coach Carlton walking toward him, he thought he knew what he was going to hear. But the coach only said quietly, "Jeremy, I couldn't figure out what was going on yesterday. You just weren't doing things the way you normally do."

Jeremy didn't know what to say. He wanted to ask why he couldn't get the green light to steal. And why the coach didn't trust him to swing the bat. But his parents had always taught him not to talk back to adults. So Jeremy said, "I just messed up."

"But you were swinging for the fence all of a sudden. You've never done that before."

"The outfielders were pulled in," Jeremy said. "I thought I could hit over them."

Coach nodded. "Okay. I see what you had in mind. But, Jeremy, you aren't going to get it over their heads. You just aren't big enough to do that. Even if they pull in on you, you need to place the ball—hit it in the gaps. If you swing hard, you lose your bat control."

Jeremy listened to everything the coach said, trying to be respectful, but the only words that had sunk in deep were, "You just aren't big enough." The coach had the same attitude toward him that everyone else did.

"Against the Mustangs, you need to—"

"Why don't you just let Chad play?"

The words were out before Jeremy had time to think about them. He wanted the coach to say, "No, Jeremy. You're my starting center fielder. You're faster than Chad and a better hitter."

But instead, the coach said, "Do you think the team would be better off with Chad out there?"

"I don't know." Jeremy was pretty sure that he was a better player than Chad, but he didn't want to make any big claims. "Chad's getting a lot better than he used to be," Jeremy said.

"You're right. He is. So do you think I should start him?"

"I don't know. It's up to you." That was how he really felt. He wanted to be in the starting lineup, but only if the coach thought that he deserved to be.

Coach Carlton took a long look at Jeremy. Finally, he said, "Confidence is a big part of this game. You gotta believe in yourself, Jeremy."

Jeremy wanted to say, "And *you* have to believe in me, too." But he didn't.

"Let's have a good practice today, and we'll see how things go."

Unfortunately, Jeremy had a terrible practice. It was bad enough that he couldn't do anything right. What made it worse was that no one even seemed to notice.

When Jeremy took batting practice, he kept telling himself to ease off and poke the ball in a hole somewhere. But another side of him wanted to drive one hard and show the coach that he *could* belt one over an outfielder's head.

The problem was, he only proved the coach right. He kept hitting high fly balls instead of well-placed drives.

In the outfield, Jeremy didn't say anything about Thurlow hogging the ball, but he tried to take over. He tried to run to the ball and be the one to call Thurlow off. Thurlow didn't say anything at first, but when Jeremy called for a fly and then ended up dropping it, he said, "Hey, Jeremy, I could have gotten to that one. I had a better angle."

Jeremy didn't argue. How could he? He had messed up the catch. But he hadn't made the wrong decision about it being his ball.

At the end of practice, Coach called the kids together and said, "I had a little chat with Jeremy, and we're going to shake up the lineup just a bit for this Mustangs game. I'm going to have Chad start, but I want him to play right field, not center. Thurlow, you move over to center. I'm also going to change the batting order a little, too. Robbie will lead off, and then we'll go Gloria, Thurlow, Wilson, Trent, Tracy, just the way we have. Chad will bat seventh, before Adam and Ollie."

Jeremy felt like the wind had been knocked out of him. He waited for someone to say, "No, Coach. We need Jeremy out there." But no one said a word, and when the coach let the kids go, they all walked off in their little groups of two and three.

Jeremy got on his bike and rode home.

For the next two days Jeremy kept e-mailing his cousin and getting no response. He did go to the batting cages to hit a few balls each day, but he didn't see any of the other players. On Friday, he didn't go to the game until it was almost time for it to start. As he walked up, the coach glanced at him, but he didn't chew him out for missing the warm-up.

"If we can beat the Mustangs," Coach Carlton was telling the players, "we pull into a tie with them for the second-half lead. But if we lose, we're two games back. So this is the biggest game of the season for us. The Mustangs have the best record in the league, but I know we can do it."

The players responded to that. They all yelled that they would do it this time. They seemed a lot more excited than they had been against the Whirlwinds.

Jeremy listened from behind the others, then

turned and walked toward the dugout. Adam trotted by him and then stopped and looked around. "Hey, Jeremy, how come you came so late? You didn't get a chance to warm up."

"What difference does it make? I'll be sitting around for five or six innings anyway."

"Hey, you gotta be ready to go. The coach might put you in at any time."

Jeremy shrugged.

Adam looked surprised, or maybe confused. "What's going on, Jeremy? You've always had a great attitude."

"I'll be ready when he puts me in," Jeremy said. And he was determined he would be. When he got in the game, he wanted to make some things happen. He needed to *show* the coach that he deserved to be in the starting lineup.

The Mustangs were up first, so the Scrappers took the field. Ollie warmed up to pitch. He looked good, too. He kept talking softly, but he had learned to listen to himself without speaking so loudly that everyone else could hear. And maybe something about the strange distant look on his face, and his constant mumbling, was scary to the batters.

Billy Mauer, the Mustangs' leadoff hitter, took a couple of pitches. He was probably hoping to get ahead in the count and put the pressure on Ollie to throw strikes. But he ended up with a 1 and 1 count, and then he swung and missed on a red-hot fastball.

He dug in and got ready for another one, but Ollie pulled the string and tossed a great change-up. Billy started to swing, held up, and looked at strike three.

Eddie Donaldson, the Mustangs' center fielder, had the same troubles and also ended up striking out.

Out in the field, the Scrappers were all talking it up, yelling to Ollie, letting the Mustangs know they had some confidence these days.

But just when Ollie seemed to have the Mustangs on the run, Sheri Gibby, their left fielder, stayed with Ollie's curve and socked it over Tracy's head into right field.

Then Alan Pingree, with his usual self-confidence, stepped into the box and swung his bat a couple of times. He waited for the pitch he wanted, and then he *killed* it. He hit the ball on a line—straight over the left field fence.

It was a powerful blow, done with ease, and Jeremy watched what it did to the Scrappers. They were still trying to keep up the chatter in the field, but all the intensity was gone. They suddenly sounded as though they were trying to convince themselves.

Maybe two runs were nothing to worry about, but everyone knew how tough the Mustangs were. Getting behind in the first inning was the last thing anyone had wanted to do.

Ollie seemed all right, though. Early in the season, he might have fallen apart after a shot like that, but now, he walked off the mound and had a chat with himself. Then he threw a great pitch, hard and down, and Snake Stabler hit a feeble little grounder to Gloria, who gunned him down.

The Scrappers tried to fire themselves back up as they ran in from the field. "Let's get those runs back right now," Thurlow shouted, and he was one guy who meant business. He was not usually a cheerleader, but Jeremy could see how badly he wanted to win this game.

But Justin Lou was pitching for the Mustangs, and he was popping the ball pretty well. He was not the Mustangs' number one pitcher, but he was developing his power. He looked a lot better than he had earlier in the season.

Robbie usually didn't make a lot of mistakes at bat, but Lou's fastball was sneaky fast, and Robbie swung late at a pitch and popped it up. The ball was foul and looked like it was heading for the bleachers, but Pingree ran from his first base position, leaned over the fence, and made the catch.

Gloria, however, was ready for Lou's fastball—which seemed to explode from a short, simple windup. She took that level swing of hers and met the ball, solid. The ball jumped into left field before Stabler could take a step to flag it down. Gibby, out in left, got the ball in quickly and held Gloria to a single, but now Thurlow was coming up, and this was the Scrappers' chance to show they could match the Mustangs run for run, homer for homer.

Thurlow looked calm on the surface, but Jeremy knew how eager he was. When he took his stance, he looked like a panther ready to spring on its prey. The first pitch was up, but Thurlow ripped at it—and got nothing.

"That's all right, Thurlow. Find the one you want," Coach Carlton yelled.

Jeremy couldn't believe it. When Jeremy had swung at a high one, the coach had gotten on him for swinging at bad pitches.

The next pitch was probably outside, but Thurlow chased it. He fouled it off to the right side.

"Come on, Thurlow. Wait for a good one."

But the coach didn't sound as upset as he did when Jeremy chased a bad pitch. He trusted Thurlow.

Thurlow let a couple of pitches go by and forced Lou to come back with something in the strike zone.

But Lou threw a great pitch—a change-up just when Thurlow was looking for more hard stuff. Thurlow tried to check his swing, but it was too late. He foul tipped the ball, and Brandon Flowers, the catcher, hung on for strike three.

Jeremy felt the air go out of the team. Wilson had some good cuts at the ball, but he finally struck out, too. The Scrappers weren't making much noise when they ran back to the field to start the second inning.

CHAPTER FIVE

"Come on, now," Coach Carlton yelled to the players. "We're all right. Just hold 'em to those two runs, and we'll be okay."

Wanda was standing next to Coach Carlton. She gave a high-pitched whoop and then called to Ollie, "You keep firing. We're going to get these guys today."

Jeremy saw the players pick up the talk, and Gloria yelled, "Hey, Gomer, wave a white flag and maybe Ollie will go easy on you."

Stein, the kid everyone called "Gomer," grinned at Gloria. Then, almost as though he had done it on purpose, he slammed the first pitch hard on the ground, right at her.

Gloria got down on the ball, fielded it

perfectly, took a good stride, and threw the ball . . . out of sight.

The ball had slipped from her fingers—or somehow gotten away from her—and her throw was way over Adam's outstretched glove. Gomer made the turn and cruised over to second.

Once he reached the base, Gloria walked away, but Gomer was giving her a work over, and Gloria was clearly mad enough to rip his big ears off.

But she didn't say a word. She simply slugged her glove and then blew a big, pink bubble. That was to say, "I'm not worried," but Jeremy thought she did look a little concerned. The team couldn't afford to let Gomer score and build the lead to three.

All the Scrappers were a lot quieter now.

Derek Salinas, who usually pitched for the Mustangs, was playing right field today. He was up next. But he popped the ball up, almost straight in the air, and Wilson got under it and made the catch. Gomer had to stay at second.

That brought up Flowers, the catcher. He was a big guy, and he could knock the ball a long way if he connected. But Ollie got a pitch in on his hands, and Flowers hit a little rainbow that arced out to Adam. Adam took it for the out.

Two outs, and now the threat of a big inning seemed over. Jeremy was still feeling bad that he wasn't out there, but he was trying to support the players. He still hoped for a big win today. And he hoped to get in the game soon.

Lou was up, and he was a lousy hitter. He knocked a soft grounder toward Tracy, and Jeremy was sure the Scrappers were out of trouble. But the ball took a strange bounce, flattened out, and scooted low, right under her glove. It rolled between her legs and on into right field.

Thurlow charged hard, but by the time he got to the ball, Gomer had scored.

Tracy walked back to the infield with her hands on her hips. She was obviously disgusted with herself. "That's all right. You got a bad hop, that's all," the coach said.

But Jeremy knew there was more to it than that. Tracy should have been down lower, to block the ball. Why was it the coach was tougher on Jeremy than he was anyone else?

Ollie was looking up at Mount Timpanogos. Jeremy just hoped he wouldn't lose his cool. He had pitched really well, and two errors had caused his problems this inning.

The top of the order was up now. Mauer was a scooter. He often hit the ball on the ground and then pressured the infielders with his speed. The last thing the Scrappers needed now was another error.

Ollie threw a pretty good pitch, but not a real stinger. Mauer hit the ball on the ground all right, but it was a hot shot past Robbie. Robbie dived for it, but too late. Trent cut the ball off and got it back in quickly. Lou had to stop at second, but now the Mustangs had another threat going.

"Two outs," Robbie yelled to everyone. "We're all right. Let's get this guy."

Donaldson looked bad on the first pitch, bailing out as he swung at a ball inside. But then he came back with a good stroke and slammed the next pitch up the middle for another single.

Lou didn't have much speed, so the coach held him up, but now the bases were loaded and the game seemed on the line. The Scrappers knew they couldn't afford to let the Mustangs have a big inning.

Ollie was still talking to himself. He seemed a little upset, but he showed no signs of panic. He threw a couple of hard shots past Gibby, and she didn't move her bat. She was down 0 and 2, and Jeremy was thinking, *Just one more strike*.

But she stuck her bat in the way of the next pitch, and the ball floated toward Adam. It seemed a sure out, but he charged toward it and couldn't reach it. It hit in the dirt and took a crazy bounce toward the mound. Adam and Ollie both ran after it and almost slammed into each other.

Tracy hustled over to cover the bag and got there in time, but Ollie picked up the ball and tried to flip it too quickly. It bounced in the dirt and then glanced off Tracy's glove.

Another run scored.

The play was no one's fault. Ollie had made a great pitch. The ball had simply had a lot of spin on it—and had bounced funny again. But it felt as though everything was going to pieces. Now the score was 4 to 0, and the bases were still loaded.

Worse yet, Pingree was up to bat.

The guy was so easygoing. He looked like he was playing a game of "work up" in some vacant lot. He paid no attention to all the yelling. He just stood at the plate, watched the first pitch go by for a strike, took his stance again, and then laced the next pitch into right field.

Thurlow turned on the afterburners and almost got to the ball, but it bounded past him. And Chad wasn't fast enough to give him any help. Jeremy knew that if he had been in center and Thurlow in right, one of them would have at least cut it off.

It would have been a hit either way, but now the ball was rolling all the way to the fence. By the time Thurlow got to it and threw it to the infield, all three runners had scored.

The score was now 7 to 0, and the Scrappers were being humiliated. Over in the other dugout, the Mustangs were shouting and celebrating. Someone said, "This one's for the championship, and the Scrappers didn't even *show up* today."

There wasn't much arguing about that.

Stabler did hit a fly ball to Trent for the final

out of the inning, but that didn't seem to matter much at the moment.

The players walked to the dugout, all with their heads down. But Coach Carlton got on them for that. "Hey, we can score seven runs just as fast as they can. This game isn't over."

Gloria tossed her glove against the fence and yelled, "Come on, you guys. We're not this bad."

Tracy said, "You know what Flowers just told me? He said, 'Salinas could have started today, but the coach saved him for the next game. We don't need our best pitcher to beat you guys.'"

"Hey, we aren't going to take that," Robbie said. "Let's make it happen, right now."

Jeremy liked the feeling. He didn't say anything himself, but he sensed the team was getting fired up, not down on one another. No one mentioned the errors, the bad luck; they just talked about getting going.

Trent was up first, and he hadn't been saying much, but Jeremy saw how serious he was. He watched Lou's first pitch, outside. Then, when Lou came with a pitch over the plate, Trent's bat

Lou came with a pitch over the plate, Trent's bat exploded into the ball. He drove a bullet of a line drive past the shortstop and . . .

But no! The Snake twisted and stabbed with his glove—and caught the ball!

All the Scrappers jumped to their feet. They could hardly believe that Stabler had made the catch. It should have ripped his glove off.

But he recovered his balance and held the ball up for everyone to see. Then he looked at the Scrappers' dugout and laughed. He tossed the ball to Lou.

The Mustangs were all roaring. Who could blame them?

Trent walked back to the dugout. He was shaking his head. The Scrappers' new determination was seeping away like air from a punctured tire.

Jeremy knew that Tracy wanted to do something good to lift the team, but she topped a ball and sent it scooting back to Lou. Lou threw her out before she was halfway down the line.

Now Chad was up. What Jeremy could see immediately was that Chad was looking for a walk. He let two called strikes go by and then finally swung and missed a pitch that was almost in the dirt.

Jeremy was pretty sure the coach would put him in for Chad soon. Something had to change right away.

But the coach didn't make a change, and the third inning produced nothing for either team.

Ollie was still throwing well, and he got the Mustangs out in the top of the fourth, too. But as Gloria said, as she got ready to head for the plate, "All right, guys, we can't wait any longer. We've *got* to get some runs this inning."

When she took her stance at the plate, she looked like a bulldog—eager to eat someone's leg off. But she surprised everyone by squaring off and dropping a bunt down the first base line. Flowers ran after the ball, but it rolled ahead of him, and Pingree stayed back, hoping Flowers could make the play.

Flowers finally caught up to the ball, but not soon enough. Gloria had already whizzed past first.

The Mustangs made fun of Gloria, bunting

for a hit, but it was a smart play, and it fired up the Scrappers. They might have to scrap for some runs, but they weren't going to give up without a fight.

Thurlow used his head this time, too. Lou was being careful with him, pitching him outside, so Thurlow let the first one go by. When Lou got one over the plate, Thurlow was ready. He took that quick swing of his and *smacked* the ball.

He hit a shot as long as any Jeremy had ever seen. It cleared the fence and some big spruce trees well beyond the fence. It was a major-league shot, and the Scrappers finally had something to go wild about.

They ran out and greeted Gloria and Thurlow as they crossed the plate, giving them high fives. Both of them were saying the same thing. "That's only two. Let's get some more."

But Wilson tried to hit another long one, and he struck out. Then Trent got good wood on the ball but flied out to center field. After that, Tracy hit a ground ball that seemed headed for right. Donaldson, however, cut to his left and made a great pickup. Then he flipped the ball to

Pingree, and the inning was over.

The Mustangs were good, and they hadn't gotten rattled when the Scrappers finally showed some life. Jeremy wondered. Maybe the better team *was* winning—not only the game but also the championship standings. The Scrappers were still down 7 to 2, and time was running out.

CHAPTER SIX

Pingree was up.

At least no one was on base. If he hit another bomb, only one run would score. But Ollie pitched him well this time, had him 1 and 2, when Pingree reached out and poked the ball to the opposite field. He dropped the ball in front of Chad and had himself a single.

Jeremy had to hand it to the guy. He took what he got from the pitcher, and he always seemed to make something happen. Jeremy just hoped this wouldn't be the start of another big inning for the Mustangs.

When Stabler lashed a single to left, it looked like that was exactly what was going to happen.

Two on, and Gomer was coming up. The guy was a good hitter.

Jeremy had seen this happen so many times this year. Ollie would start strong, but then he would lose some of his speed, some of his confidence, and things would go badly for him after that.

Ollie had another chat with himself. When he turned around, Jeremy could see that he was not going to back off this time. He hadn't lost his will to win. He put a perfect pitch on the inside of the plate and over the knees. Gomer tried to go down after the ball and hit a little roller back to the mound.

Ollie made the stop and spun toward third base. Robbie had broken to the bag and was ready for the throw. Ollie rifled the ball to him and got the force on the lead runner.

"That's the way," Coach Carlton yelled. "Keep it up."

Ollie stepped back to the rubber and took his signal from Wilson. Salinas got ready. Ollie gave the pitch a big motion, but he threw a breaking ball. Salinas took an awkward swing and sent a slow bouncer to the left side of second base.

Gloria broke to her left, but she had to dive to snag the ball. Salinas seemed to have himself an infield hit. But Gloria rolled over and, still on the ground, flipped the ball toward second base.

Tracy was coming hard, and Gloria had led her perfectly. Tracy caught the ball in her bare hand, stepped on the bag, and jumped. As she spun in the air, she got everything she could on her throw to first. The ball looped toward first, but it bounced in the dirt in front of Adam. Adam stayed with it and dug it out on the short hop.

Out at second! Out at first!

It was not just a double play. It was big-league stuff. Jeremy jumped up and cheered. When he glanced toward the Mustangs' bench, he saw the Mustangs' coach clapping his hands and nodding. And then he heard Gomer yell to Gloria, "Hey, nice play."

"Now we're playing some real baseball," Coach Carlton yelled.

This was great. Maybe the coach would put Jeremy in the game for Chad now. But Chad got a bat and walked to the plate. The coach didn't call him back. And when he took the first pitch for a ball, the coach yelled, "That's it. Good eye."

Chad was up there to do what Jeremy had always done in the past: find a way to get on.

Lou's next pitch was over the plate, and still Chad didn't swing. Chances were, he wouldn't swing at all, and Lou had to know that.

But Lou missed high and then low, and then he tried to aim one and took too much off the pitch. It dropped low again and Chad was on base.

Everyone was yelling, "Way to go, Chad. Good eye. Way to work him."

But Lou was mad at himself for walking Chad. He fired some good pitches, and Adam went down swinging. Then Ollie tried way too hard to make something happen. He took a couple of swings at bad pitches. He struck out, too. Suddenly the budding rally, with the leadoff guy on, seemed over before it had really begun.

But Robbie had Lou's number. He let an inside fastball go by and then laid off a curve, even though it broke in the zone for a strike. He was looking for speed again, and he got it on the next pitch. His stroke was smooth as satin, and he *crunched* the ball. It didn't sail as long as Thurlow's big blow, but it made it over the same left field fence.

Two more runs scored. Now the Scrappers were getting back in the game. The score was 7 to 4. And with Gloria and Thurlow coming up, maybe the inning wasn't over.

Lou wasn't going to give Gloria anything she could pull. He kept the ball on the outside of the plate—or beyond. On a 2 and 1 count, Gloria finally strode toward the plate, reached out, and stroked the ball down the right field line. She didn't get it all, but she hit it hard enough to send it bouncing all the way into the corner. She ran hard around the bases and went into third, standing up.

Thurlow clearly wanted to hit another one out. Jeremy could see that. One more long one, and the Scrappers were almost there. Thurlow didn't swing at the outside stuff Lou was sticking to. But when Lou finally tried to bust him inside, Thurlow released on the ball and pulled it to the left side. The ball shot past the third baseman for a solid single, and Gloria scored from third.

Gibby fielded the ball and threw hard toward

the cutoff. Thurlow must have thought the ball was going home, because he broke for second. But there was no chance to get Gloria, so the catcher yelled, "Cut!" Stabler reached up and caught the ball, turned, and tossed the ball to second. Anyone else would have been out, but Thurlow got there in a flash, and he slid under the tag.

Safe!

Lou was clearly shaken. He took some time before he threw his first pitch to Wilson, but he was losing some of his control. He was still trying to pitch everyone away, and he threw one too many outside—and walked Wilson.

Trent was stroking the ball a lot better these days. He looked sure of himself as he stepped into the box.

Lou knew he had to throw strikes. The first pitch was down the middle, and Trent whacked it straight over the pitcher's head.

Thurlow raced around third and dug for home. Again, the play was close, but Thurlow outran the ball, made a perfect hook slide, and scored the run. It was 7 to 6, and the Scrappers were still scrapping! All the players in the dugout were going crazy.

The runners had gone to second and third on the throw. Now Cindy, in the game for Tracy, had a chance to put the Scrappers in front.

She waited for a good pitch, too, and she stroked it perfectly. But she hit it right at Donaldson, in center field. He made the catch, and the side was finally retired.

The Scrappers hadn't quite made it over the hill, but they had come a long way. Now it was time to play some tough defense again. That meant the coach *had* to be thinking about putting Jeremy back on the field, but Coach Carlton didn't make the change. Jeremy could hardly believe it.

Flowers was up first. He hit a high fly ball to right. It was an easy out—maybe. Chad was out there, and Jeremy always feared the worst with him. He ran back a little, then in a little, and finally had to drop back fast again. But he stuck his glove up, and the ball dropped in—and stayed.

All the players were yelling, "Good catch. Way to go, Chad." Jeremy knew that he or Thurlow would have made the play look easy.

The worst thing was listening to Mr. Corrigan roar, "You're the man, Chad. Way to be there."

Lou also flied out, but this time to Trent, who made the play look a whole lot easier.

Mauer, however, fouled off five or six pitches before he got a pitch in the dirt for ball four. Then a tall kid, a sub for Donaldson, came in and stood there while Ollie tried to throw strikes. He ended up with a walk, too. Jeremy was pretty sure that Ollie's meltdown time had finally come.

But a new guy was in the game for Gibby, and he thought he would wait out Ollie, too—especially with the coach screaming, "Make him throw strikes."

Ollie threw three, and the sub only swung at the last one. And missed. The Scrappers had held up once again. They just needed to scratch out a couple more runs. And they had two more chances to do just that.

In the bottom of the sixth, Lou found some re-newed strength against Chad and Martin, who was now in the game for Adam. Both of them struck out.

Just when the inning seemed over, Ollie hit a double, and Robbie hit a hard shot on the ground to Mauer. He muffed the ball and then made a late throw to first. With two on, Lou got too careful again and walked Gloria.

Now Thurlow had another chance. The bases were loaded, and the biggest win of the year was within reach. All the Scrappers in the dugout were going nuts.

On the first pitch, Thurlow took one of his lashing swings and made contact. A cheer went up, but Jeremy knew from the sound of the bat that Thurlow hadn't connected the way he needed to. It was just a long out. The left fielder made the catch, and the Scrappers had left the bases full.

The players all collapsed on the bench for a moment before they realized that they had to go back onto the field. They tried to start talking it up again, but there wasn't much noise left in them.

One thing *was* obvious. The coach had to put Jeremy in the game now. That was his rule, that everyone played.

"Go back to center field, but bat for Cindy," Coach Carlton told him. "Thurlow is moving to right and Chad to second base."

Jeremy trotted out to the field. He finally had his chance to do something that would make a difference.

Ollie seemed to be reaching back for something extra now. He struck out Pingree and got Stabler on an easy grounder. But then Gomer stroked a long drive toward the gap to right. Jeremy instantly saw that it was a hard shot, and he took off fast. He angled for the ball and was moving into range when he heard Thurlow yell, "Mine!" So Jeremy backed off, and Thurlow made the catch.

Everyone yelled to Thurlow, told him what a great catch he had made, but Jeremy was steaming. Thurlow had to show off like that every time. Jeremy could have made the catch—*should* have.

At least he knew he was going to get up in the bottom of the seventh. He was batting third. He had one more chance to come through.

Wilson was up first, and he had the power to tie the game with a swing. Everyone was chanting, "Go, Wilson! Go, Wilson," as he walked to the plate.

The first pitch was outside, but Wilson tried to pull it. He hit the ball off the end of his bat, and it squirted out to first base, where Pingree picked it up and stepped on the bag.

Trent was more patient. He worked the

count to 3 and 2, then fouled one off. But he swung and missed on a pitch that might have been ball four.

Jeremy felt the Scrappers give up—lose their last bit of hope. Even if Jeremy stayed alive, Chad was coming up after him. There was no reason to expect anything good to happen.

But Jeremy was going to do something right today. He watched the first pitch closely, thought about poking it, but laid off and got the call. Ball one.

The pitch had been close, and Lou was a little angry. Jeremy liked to see that. The next pitch had some mustard on it, but it was up high, ball two.

"That's it. Way to watch," Coach Carlton called.

But Jeremy wanted a hit. The next pitch was down the center, and Jeremy took an easy swing and looped the ball to the right side. The substitute right fielder was playing back. He came running in, but the ball bounced in front of him, and Jeremy was on.

"That's the stuff!" the coach yelled. "Come on, Chad, keep it going."

But what were the chances? Even if Chad somehow got a hit, then Martin would be at bat. With the weakest part of the Scappers' order coming up, Jeremy needed to get into scoring position.

On the first pitch to Chad, Lou hardly gave Jeremy a look. The pitch was a strike, and Chad's hopes for a walk were not great.

Why wasn't the coach signaling for a steal? If he could get to second, he could score on a single, maybe even a throwing error. It was the best chance they had.

Jeremy led off the base and watched the coach. No signal.

Lou gave him a brief look, but then turned and fired. Strike two.

Now he had to go. It was the Scappers' last hope. Maybe the catcher would throw the ball into center field. Anything was better than depending on Chad.

So Jeremy stretched his lead, watched for his chance to go.

Then suddenly, Lou jerked his foot from the rubber and made his move to first.

Jeremy was caught and he knew it.

He broke for second, but he had no chance. Pingree took the throw from Lou and then tossed the ball to Mauer, who put the tag on Jeremy as he slid into second.

The game was over, and the Scrappers had lost. Jeremy stayed on the ground. He didn't want to get up.

CHAPTER SEVEN

Coach Carlton wanted to talk to the team. Jeremy wanted to leave and not face his teammates, but as he tried to slip away, Coach said, "Come here for a minute, Jeremy." He didn't sound mad, but Jeremy was pretty sure he was.

Mr. Corrigan wasn't hiding how *he* felt. He asked Chad, "What did that little kid think he was doing?" At least he spoke in his soft voice. Maybe a few people in town didn't hear him.

"Kids," Coach said, "you got off to a bad start today, but you made a great comeback. I was proud of the way you hung in there. We came pretty close to getting them this time."

Jeremy looked around. All he could see was gloom. The Scrappers' chance for the championship was all but gone.

"I guess what pleases me most," the coach

continued, "is that early in the season, we hardly looked like a baseball team, and today we looked as good as the Mustangs. We had some bad luck in one inning and didn't play our best, but after that, we competed. Ollie kept throwing well all the way to the end, and you kids kept chipping away at the lead."

"It doesn't matter. We can't win the championship now," Gloria said.

"Well, first off, it does matter. Even if we don't take first place, all you kids have come a long way. So that's important. But also, we aren't about to give up on this season. We've got to beat the Pit Bulls next week, and who knows, maybe someone will knock off the Mustangs."

"They'd have to lose twice," Robbie said.

"Well, that could happen. But we can't control that. What we can do is beat the Pit Bulls, and then go after the next one. Maybe the Mustangs think they have it now, and maybe they'll let up a little. You never know."

But there were no cheers. Not even the parents were saying anything encouraging. Jeremy didn't think it was so terrible to come in second;

he just wished he hadn't been the guy to mess up at the end.

"Here's one thing that worries me," Coach Carlton said. "We seem to be looking for that big hit—a home run—all the time. If one of you gets good wood on the ball and knocks it out, that's fine. But not everyone is a home run hitter. We need to do a better job of moving runners—with a bunt or by hitting behind the runner. We need to think more about bat control, putting the ball where no one is—instead of swinging for the fence all the time."

"Home runs kept us in the game," Wilson said.

"That's true. But if we could have played things right and figured out a way to get one more run—with some teamwork—we would still be playing out there right now. So tomorrow at practice, that's what we're going to be working on: moving runners, finding a way to score that extra run."

The coach let everyone go. Jeremy wanted to talk to him, in a way, at least say he was sorry for getting himself picked off. But Coach Carlton didn't say anything to him—no one did.

Jeremy knew what that meant. They all thought he had done something stupid. Maybe the team hadn't had much of a chance, but Jeremy had ruined what little chance there had been.

So Jeremy got on his bike and rode home. He sat down at his computer, turned it on, and waited for it to boot up. Then he checked his e-mail. He was glad to see that he finally had a message from his cousin Eddy:

Hey, Jer,

Sorry I didn't get back to you sooner. We went up to Palmdale for a couple of days to visit Aunt Charlotte and Uncle Hal. They have a pool, but it was still pretty boring. In fact, the whole thing turned into a mess. On the way back our car broke down. It stopped running right on the freeway. We had to wait for a tow truck, and it must have been a hundred degrees out there. Then, after we waited about two hours, the mechanic said it was only a belt that had broken. I guess it was one that goes around everything—the air conditioner and power steering and all that stuff. One little belt, and it messed up our whole day.

Anyway, I'm back now, so write back to me. I hope baseball is going better. I missed one of my games while I was gone, and my team finally won a game. Maybe there's a connection—do you think?

Later, Eddy

Jeremy smiled. Eddy really wasn't much of a ballplayer. But he had said something in his message that hit Jeremy—something he wanted to think about.

All evening Jeremy kept thinking about that belt that probably didn't cost much, didn't seem very important, but kept an engine running. Maybe that had nothing to do with baseball, but Jeremy thought he was finally understanding something about himself.

At practice the next morning Jeremy could see that the Scrappers had given up hope and were just going through the motions. But Coach Carlton kept after everyone. He spent a lot of time on batting practice. He had the players—even the home run hitters—try to lay some good bunts down. And he would call out, "Now, go to right field with this next pitch. Hit behind the runner."

That was something Jeremy could do. When he went back to poking the ball, the way he had most of the year, he realized he had better bat control than most of his teammates. Time and again, he placed the ball where the coach asked him to hit it. And the coach was impressed.

"See that, kids," he said. "There may be times when you swing for the long ball, but you're not true hitters until you have the kind of bat control Jeremy has."

A true hitter? Jeremy could hardly believe the coach was talking about him. He was the singles hitter. The walker.

Jeremy really worked on his fielding, too. He tried to take control of the outfield, call for the ball if it was his, and recognize that Thurlow could get to some balls that he couldn't. Above all, he tried to use his head, draw a bead on the ball before he took off after it.

Jeremy made more noise than usual, too. He was trying to build some enthusiasm. Maybe the team didn't have much of a chance for the championship now, but the coach was right. The Scrappers had to win their games one at a time and see what happened. Even if they didn't win the big first-place trophy, they could come in second and not just blow away the rest of the season.

The team needed someone to step up and lead the way. Jeremy knew he wasn't the team's engine, but sometimes it was something little— like that belt Eddy had talked about—that made everything else go.

No one said anything to Jeremy about getting picked off first base in the Mustangs game. A lot of people had made mistakes; maybe they didn't think it was that big of a deal. Besides, instead of hiding away, Jeremy was talking a little more, trying to be friendly, and everyone seemed to respond to that.

After practice, Jeremy waited around. He wanted to talk to the coach—but not when anyone else was there. So he watched, and after the coach had gathered up the bats and equipment and was heading for his truck, Jeremy got on his bike and pedaled after him.

"Coach, can I talk to you?" he said.

"Sure." The coach swung the equipment bag off his shoulder and set it down. Then he took his ball cap off and wiped the sweat from his face with a big blue handkerchief he always kept in his back pocket.

"I don't like sitting on the bench," Jeremy

said. "I told you to let Chad start instead of me, but I wish I hadn't said that."

The coach grinned. He put his cap back on, then tugged on the bill, to straighten it. "What makes you think you ought to be back in the starting lineup?"

"I'm a good leadoff man. I can get on base. You just said I had good bat control. And I have a small strike zone. I can get a lot of walks."

"I know all that. But all of a sudden, against the Whirlwinds, you started trying to belt the ball out of the park."

"I know. But that was stupid."

"You *are* a good leadoff man. But sometimes, in the outfield, you get yourself in trouble."

"Thurlow ought to be in center, and I ought to be in right. He should be the one covering the most territory. I'm not overrunning balls the way I used to, but I'm always scared I'm going to mess up. If he were the one taking control, I think I could do all right."

"Well, that's funny you would say that. I've been thinking the same thing. At the first of the season—as I'm sure you noticed—Thurlow had such a bad attitude that I didn't want him in center. But he's come around now, and that's probably where he belongs. The only trouble is, I also need a strong arm in right, and Chad might have you there."

Jeremy nodded. "Coach, maybe that's right. Maybe Chad should be the starter. But don't leave me on the bench until the seventh inning. I want to play."

"Jeremy, I put you on the bench because you told me that's where you thought you belonged. I thought I'd leave you there until you showed some fight. Out there today, you looked like you wanted your position back."

"I had the wrong attitude there for a while. It's like a belt on a car engine."

"What?"

"I was mad about everyone telling me how little I am and about you telling me not to swing. So I wanted to get some big hits."

Coach Carlton looked a little confused. He probably didn't see what that had to do with a car engine. The important thing was, Jeremy saw the connection. He knew it was his atti-tude—just a little thing—that made all the dif-ference in the way he played.

"But you haven't mentioned the biggest problem, Jeremy."

Jeremy figured he knew what that was. He looked down at the ground. "I know. I took too big of a lead, and—"

"No. That's not it."

Jeremy looked up again.

The coach crossed his arms and looked rather stern. "When you start ignoring my signals, I can't work with you. Someone has to be in charge so that the whole team is working together."

"But you're teaching everyone to bunt, and you hardly ever let me steal. I have the speed to take second without having to give up an out."

The coach smiled. "You have a good grasp of this game, Jeremy. You think about it more than most kids do. That's what a leadoff batter has to do, too. But all summer, every time I gave you the green light to steal, you just took off. A good base runner watches the pitcher more carefully than that, and he considers the whole situation. Isn't that what I've been telling you?"

"At the end of the game yesterday, it made sense for me to get to second. We had weak hitters coming up. I needed to be in scoring position."

"Yes. And you led off too far and got yourself picked off. And that's not the first time you've done that this season. That's exactly what I was afraid of, so I didn't give you the steal sign."

Jeremy nodded. He had to admit the coach had a point. "Okay," he said. "I won't steal on my own from now on. I'll do what you tell me to do. And I'll watch the pitchers more."

"If you'll do that, I'll give you the green light more often—because I do want to get more aggressive on the base paths. We have some decent speed on our team, and we need to use it more."

"Okay," Jeremy said.

"I do like what you said about attitude, Jeremy. It's what makes the whole team work. I need your help in this next game. We need to get the team fired up. Everyone's really down right now."

But did that mean . . . ?

"I'm going to start you in right field—and at the leadoff position. So don't let me down."

Jeremy grinned. "Don't worry," he said. "I won't."

CHAPTER EIGHT

Jeremy was never going to be a team cheer-leader. Other players could do that. Gloria always made a lot of noise on the bench, and so did Wilson. But Jeremy made up his mind he was not going to be the silent guy at the end of the bench anymore. All weekend he thought about what he wanted to do in the game against the Pit Bulls. He was going to be more than a leadoff hitter—he was going to be a leader.

But on Tuesday evening, at game time, his nervousness was back. He didn't feel the confidence he knew he needed—that belt that was going to make the engine work. When he ran out to right field, he felt a little strange. What if he had to make a long throw, all the way to third, and showed how weak his arm was?

Still, he was talking it up more than he ever had before. "Come on, Adam. Blow 'em away," he was yelling.

What Jeremy didn't feel was the same enthusiasm from his teammates. The loss to the Mustangs had taken a lot out of them. Gloria was shouting and seemed to have her usual intensity, but most of the players were pretty quiet.

Before the game, Coach Carlton had talked about playing smart and playing together. "The Mustangs have three games left, the same as us. We can't control what they do, but we can make sure we win all three of our games and keep the pressure on them."

"They're playing the Hot Rods today, starting at the same time we are," Robbie said.

"Rohrbach's been pitching great lately," Gloria said. "The Hot Rods could beat those guys."

"That's fine," the coach said. "But don't pay any attention to that game. "What we have to do is concentrate on this one—and play the way we know we can."

The truth was, it was hard to believe that the Hot Rods had any chance of beating the

Mustangs. But now, standing in right field, Jeremy didn't think much about that. What he wanted was to get the win, and to be one of the players who made it happen.

Waxman, the Pit Bulls' quick shortstop, was leading off as usual, and he let a couple of Adam's steaming fastballs sail by, high. Then he stepped out of the batter's box and shouted to his bench, "Hey, we won't have to swing today. Adam can't throw strikes."

That, of course, was a little "psych-out"—something to get Adam upset. But Adam brought the ball down, and Jeremy, from right field, was sure he had thrown a strike. Waxman didn't swing, however, and the ump called it ball three.

"Where was that, ump?" Gloria was yelling. The umpire motioned with his hand that the ball had been low.

Maybe. But now Adam did need to throw a strike. Jeremy yelled, "No problem, Adam. Waxman can't hit. Blow it by him."

Jeremy noticed Thurlow look over at him and smile. He was probably surprised that Jeremy was yelling so much.

"That's right," Thurlow yelled. "Put it in there. Waxman can't hurt you."

Waxman was clearly taking all the way, and Adam drilled one over the center of the plate for strike one. Now the whole team picked up on the chatter that Jeremy and Thurlow had started. Trent yelled, "You got him now, Adam. Waxman can't hit your fastball."

And that's exactly what Adam threw—a fastball away. It was probably ball four, but Waxman went after it and knocked a bounding ball toward Tracy, at second. She charged the ball, took it on a big hop, then turned and tossed it over to Ollie, at first.

One away.

It was no big deal, but that 3 and 1 count could have led to trouble. And now, the team was starting to sound a little more alive. Robbie was shouting to the outfield, "All right. One down. Be ready out there."

James Wayment was up. He wasn't looking for a walk. He went after the first pitch and spanked it hard. The ball was hit on a line to right center. Jeremy took off hard. At first he thought he had the best shot at the ball, but

Thurlow was making up ground fast. He was streaking toward Jeremy.

It was obvious that neither one of them could catch the ball on the fly, but Thurlow had the best chance of cutting it off. Jeremy angled deeper and ran behind Thurlow to back him up.

Thurlow was still running all out, and at the last second he lunged, but the ball bounced past his glove.

Jeremy took another step and made his own lunge. He felt the ball stick in his glove, but he couldn't keep his feet. He stumbled and nose-dived into the grass. But as he rolled onto his side, he saw Thurlow spinning back toward him. Without getting up, he flipped the ball to Thurlow, who turned and threw hard to second base.

Wayment slid into second as Gloria took the powerful throw. The umpire called him safe, but it was close. Jeremy and Thurlow had almost pulled off a great play.

"Hey, way to run," Thurlow told Jeremy. "When I couldn't cut the ball off, I thought Wayment had a sure triple. But we almost got him at second."

"You made a great throw," Jeremy said.

"That was good thinking—to toss it to me."

Jeremy thought so, too. And the coach was yelling, "Way to work together out there."

The team was fired up even more now. Maybe they had given up a double, but the all-out effort seemed to get the Scrappers excited. Everyone was yelling, even Chad.

Jeremy had thought that Chad wouldn't like having to go back to the bench, but he had whispered to Jeremy, just before the team had taken the field, "I didn't like starting. It made me too nervous. My dad doesn't like it, but it's okay with me."

Lumps Lanman came up after that, and Jeremy worried that he might crunch one and get the game off to a bad start. But he hit the ball on the ground. Gloria broke to her left and made a good pickup. Then she looked Wayment back to second and threw Lanman out at first.

Clark Krieger, a left-hander and another long-ball hitter, stepped into the box. Jeremy moved a little more toward the line in right and dropped back several steps. Krieger took one pitch and then hit a fly ball straight at Jeremy.

Jeremy took one quick step forward and then

stopped himself long enough to see that the ball was carrying well. He held his ground and finally came in a little way—but not so far as he had thought he would have to. He made the easy catch for out number three and ran off the field.

He felt some confidence. When he used his speed, he could help the team. When he used his head, he could help it even more.

Now Jeremy had to make something happen on offense. He got his bat, and then he watched Tony Gomez's warm-up pitches. Gomez was another pitcher who had improved a lot during the summer. Early in the season he had only had control when he didn't fire too hard, but he was getting more power on the ball now and getting it over the plate.

Jeremy stepped in a little closer than usual, crowded the plate, just to show Gomez that he meant business. Gomez threw the first pitch outside, and Jeremy took it for a ball.

So Gomez came inside with some real heat, obviously to scare Jeremy back—and to send a message. But Jeremy didn't lose his cool. He bent backward, out of the way, and took ball two.

Jeremy watched what the outfield was doing.

The fielders were playing in, especially the right fielder. It would be hard to punch the ball to the right side. If Gomez took something off the ball, Jeremy would try to pull it, maybe knock it down the line in left. But if he could keep Gomez off stride, maybe he could get the walk.

Gomez came with a hard shot over the plate. Jeremy reacted a little late, but he flicked his bat out and fouled the ball off.

"Make it be good," Coach Carlton was yelling. Jeremy understood what he was saying. The important thing was to get on base. But also, working a pitcher for a leadoff walk would often rattle him, and then he might have control problems.

But the pitch was in there. And hot. Jeremy tried to stroke it, but once again, he only got a piece of it and fouled it into the dirt.

Jeremy watched Gomez take a big breath and nod at his catcher's next sign. It seemed time for something different. Gomez had thrown four fastballs, so something off-speed was probably coming now.

Sure enough, Gomez changed up and threw a floater at the plate. The ball looked big enough to jump on and ride, but it was also high.

That was the kind of pitch Jeremy had suckered on lots of times. It was an easy pitch to mistime and pop up or miss completely. This time Jeremy stopped himself, and the pitch stayed high for ball three.

Jeremy was having fun. He dug in and got ready again. "Protect the plate," the coach was yelling. And Jeremy knew what that meant. He couldn't let strike three go by.

Gomez reared back and let go with a gunshot, down the middle. Jeremy took a short, quick swing and caught the ball perfectly—but late. It shot down the right field line, foul.

"That's the way. Keep him honest."

A foul ball could be quite a weapon, Jeremy realized. Now Gomez had to throw another strike.

And he did. This time Jeremy timed his swing better, but he got under the ball and fouled it back. He was hanging in there against some beastly pitches.

Jeremy could see some frustration in Gomez's face. He shook off a sign, and Jeremy guessed he was saying, "No. I'm not changing up again. I'm going to blow this ball past him."

And he did. He threw a bullet of a fastball

that sent shivers through Jeremy.

But it was low. Ball four. "Take your base!" the ump yelled. And Jeremy had earned it.

As Jeremy trotted down to first, he felt that he had done his job. "Hey, don't feel bad," he yelled to Gomez. "I have a very small strike zone. I'm hard to pitch to." And then he laughed.

When Jeremy reached first base, Wanda stepped over to him from her first base coach's box. "Coach told me to tell you if you got on—that you've got the green light. But use your head."

Jeremy nodded, and then he took a healthy lead. And he watched. Gomez didn't make a move. He threw his first pitch to Robbie, down and away. Ball one.

Jeremy calculated. If Gomez was going to have trouble throwing strikes, why not *walk* to second? No use taking chances. But he also wanted to see what kind of a lead he could get on the guy. So he stretched his lead one step and, with the pitch, bluffed a move to second.

Gomez went to the plate again, and this time he threw a strike.

That changed things a little. If Jeremy could

get a big lead, Gomez was a guy he could steal on. His motion was fairly slow. But Jeremy wasn't sure about his move to first. He needed to see how good it was.

So Jeremy stretched his lead just a little more. Gomez checked him closely, looked to the plate, and then threw to first. The throw was on the money, and Jeremy had to dive back. But he was safe. And that had to be Gomez's best move.

Jeremy knew what he could do now. He just had to get the right jump. But with no outs, he probably should give Robbie a chance to move him up. The worst thing he could do would be to get thrown out and take the pressure off Gomez.

So Jeremy didn't go, and the next pitch was in there. Robbie swung. He hit the ball in the air to left field. Sarah Pollick trotted in and made the catch. Jeremy had to stay at first.

Now Gloria was up, and Jeremy liked the idea of being on second for these next two batters. But Gloria swung at the first pitch and pushed the ball to the right side. Jeremy had taken a good lead, and he broke hard for second.

Gloria had obviously hoped to scoot the ball

past the second baseman and drive Jeremy around to third. But Wayment made a good play on the ball. He had no chance to get Jeremy, so he threw to first for the out.

"Nice job," Coach Carlton yelled to Gloria. And the Scrappers knew what he meant. She hadn't gotten a hit, but she had moved the runner up, and now Jeremy was in scoring position.

Gomez stayed tough. With first base open, he pitched on the edges, willing to walk Thurlow rather than give him something fat. But Thurlow didn't want to walk. He got too anxious and swung at a pitch in on his fists. He popped it up, and the inning was over.

Nothing too great had happened, but Jeremy felt good about the decisions he had made. He saw the coach talking to Thurlow, and he knew exactly what he was saying. The Scrappers were playing it smart today. Remember?

CHAPTER NINE

Adam was looking good—but not great. He walked Dave Boone to start the second, but then he overpowered his cousin, Stan Pfitzer, and struck him out. Pollick struck out, too, but Jon Jackson hit a line drive to left field for a single. Still, Adam threw a good pitch to Tony Gomez and got another fly-ball out, so he escaped without giving up a run, and there was still no score.

And that's how things went for a time. Gomez looked great in the bottom of the second and put away the Scrappers without much trouble. Adam struggled a little in the top of the third, but held the fort. Then the bottom of the third inning started better for the Scrappers. Adam led off with a clean single up the middle.

The Scrappers were up and yelling. Even though the game had been frustrating so far, Jeremy felt the spirit of the team building. The players did want to win—no matter what happened to the Mustangs.

But Ollie tried to bunt one of Gomez's hotshot fastballs and popped it up. Jackson, the catcher, had to rush to the backstop, but he made the catch.

The excitement in the dugout dropped off considerably. Jeremy walked to the plate feeling, once again, that he had to be the guy to make something happen.

He took a long look at the coach before he stepped into the box. There was no bunt on now, but Jeremy knew he had to move the runner to second, even if he didn't get on base.

He laid off the first pitch, and it was down the middle. Jackson laughed as he threw the ball back to Gomez. "See. Tony can hit any strike zone—even yours."

"Once," Jeremy said. The next pitch was high, and he figured he would test Gomez to see whether he could get the ball over the plate again.

Gomez checked Adam but knew very well

he wasn't going anywhere, not as slow as he was. Then he came with a curveball. Jeremy was sure the pitch had broken outside for ball two, but the umpire said, "Strike!"

Now Gomez had the edge, 1 and 2, and Jeremy had to do something. He guessed that more hard stuff was coming—and he was right. He watched the pitch, saw it was close to the plate, and he simply reached out and poked it to the right side. It wasn't a bunt, but it had the same effect. It rolled down the line and forced Krieger, the first baseman, to make the play. Gomez ran to cover first, and Krieger flipped the ball back to him. Jeremy's speed made the play close, but he was out.

So there were two away. But Adam was on second now, and Coach Carlton was yelling, "Good job, Jeremy. Way to move him over. All right now, Robbie, bring him home."

Jeremy wished he had been able to slam the ball past first base, done something to get a great inning going. But he had been feeling overpowered by Gomez's fastball, so he was glad that something good, if not great, had come of his at bat.

As Jeremy ran b... bie, he could see that ... dugout, past Rob- about *anyone's* fastball. He stepp... wasn't worried hard cut at the first pitch, and missed. ...nd took a

"Come on, now," Coach yelled. "Don't be swinging wild. Just bring Adam home."

The next pitch was in there again, but this time Robbie took an easier swing. He caught the ball flush and drove it to center field. Waxman broke to his left—and back. He ran all out and reached up for the ball, but it was over his glove. It rolled to the fence. Adam thundered around third and headed home to put the Scrappers on the scoreboard. Robbie stopped at second.

Now Gloria was up with a chance to get another run home—or two. But she was pressing a little too much. She took some hard swings and finally struck out on a nasty curveball that was breaking outside as she swung.

The third inning was over, and the game had a long way to go, but at least the Scrappers had gotten to Gomez a little and they were ahead 1 to 0. Now Adam had to keep holding the Pit Bulls.

He did just that in the fourth, but the

Scrappers didn't . . . ither, and then, in the
fifth, Wayme up, with no one on, and he
hit a fly . . . that looked like an easy out. But the
ball was up in a pretty good breeze, and it just
kept carrying. Trent ran all the way back to the
fence and waited, then he leaped. He got his
glove on the ball, but he couldn't hang on to it. It
dropped over the fence for a home run.

Wayment had gotten *so* lucky. If the ball had
been an inch or two shorter, it would have been
an out instead of a run.

But there was no changing that. The score
was 1 to 1, and it stayed that way. The Scrappers
were scratching, and they kept getting runners
into scoring position, but no one could come
through with the big hit. When the sixth inning
began, the score was still tied with one run each.

Adam had thrown a lot of pitches for a low-
scoring game, and he had pitched under a lot of
pressure, getting out of one jam after another.
But he was still throwing hard, and he hadn't
given up many walks—the way he had done
earlier in the season.

He started out well in the sixth, too, striking

out Boone on a good fastball on the outside edge. Then Egan, who was in the game for Stan Pfitzer, grounded out to Tracy, and it seemed the inning was going to be an easy one for Adam.

But Morgan Roberts, substituting for Pollick, got lucky. He swung and missed a low fastball that actually hit the plate, glanced off Wilson's glove, and off his chest protector. It was strike three, but Wilson had muffed the catch.

Roberts took off for first, and Wilson chased after the ball. He came up throwing, hard, but he rushed his throw more than he really needed to and threw high, over Ollie's head.

Roberts had struck out . . . and now he was racing over to second base. He might as well have hit a double.

Jeremy couldn't believe it. This whole game had been like that. With any luck at all, the Scrappers would have been ahead by several runs. Now the Pit Bulls had a chance to get on top.

Jackson stepped up to the plate with all his teammates screaming, "Make 'em pay for it. Give the ball a ride."

And he did. He hit the stuffing out of the ball, drove it so far over the left field fence that Trent didn't have to go back and jump this time. He just watched it go.

With one swing of the bat, the score was suddenly 3 to 1. Jeremy looked around and saw all the Scrappers kicking the dirt or staring off into space. They all looked like they had just given up on the season.

"All right. Let's get this guy. We'll get the runs back," Jeremy yelled.

Maybe no one believed it, but they all started shouting the same thing. And Adam did get Gomez to rap a high fly into short right.

Jeremy had to run a long way for the ball—finally into foul territory. But he got under it and made the catch. And after, as he was running back to the dugout, he realized that he had not been worried. He had *expected* to make the play. He was trusting in his own ability, and it was making all the difference.

In the dugout, the players were looking more angry than determined. But now was the time to break loose. Gloria, Thurlow, and Wilson were coming up, and they were the right ones to get the job done.

Just as Gloria was finding her bat, Cindy's mother came to the back of the dugout, leaned against the wire fence, and said, "Hey, kids, the Mustangs and the Hot Rods are starting the seventh inning, and the Hot Rods are ahead, 3 to 1."

There was a moment of disbelief, and then a cheer went up from the Scrappers. Jeremy looked up to see everyone in the bleachers look over. Then the word started to spread to the Scrappers' fans in the bleachers—and then on around to the other dugout.

Suddenly, everything was different. This game had always been a "must win," but now the possibilities were exciting. The Scrappers just couldn't let this one get away.

Gloria *ran* to the plate and shouted to Gomez, "Look out. Here I come."

But she didn't get too eager. She let him throw a teaser for a ball, in a little tight, and then she got the pitch she wanted and whacked it over the shortstop's head. Base hit.

Thurlow came up with everyone in the crowd screaming for a home run. But he had been swinging for the fences too much lately. He waited for a good pitch, and he drove the ball straight past the pitcher and into center. Another single.

Gloria had taken off with the crack of the bat, and she raced around to third.

Runners at the corners and no outs. Jeremy felt sure the Scrappers were starting on a rampage. He just hoped he could get in on it.

But Wilson wasn't quite as patient. He swung at an inside pitch, hit it off the handle of his bat, and popped it up. Gomez ran in and caught the ball, and the runners had to hold.

Chad had come into the game, but he was playing for Trent, not Jeremy. What scared Jeremy was that Chad might strike out, and the runners would be stuck where they were.

Chad looked nervous, probably scared of the same thing. But he knew better than to take wild swings in a situation like this. He took a couple of balls, probably started to think about walking, and got a strike. Then he took a soft swing and dropped the ball over the second baseman's head.

It was perfectly placed. It settled in for a single, and Gloria scored. Thurlow, with his speed, cruised easily around to third.

Chad grinned and clapped his hands, and his father made the whole park shake with his booming voice. "Way to go, Chad. Way to show 'em what you can do."

Jeremy was shouting, too. He was proud of Chad. The guy had come through right when he had to. Now, Tracy had to get the score tied.

Gomez was sweating hard, taking more time between pitches, and clearly he was losing some of the power off his fastball. But he was still tough. Jeremy hoped for another hit, or even some luck—an error, a walk, something.

Tracy waited for the first pitch, and then, once again, she did what the coach had been teaching the kids to do. She took a nice stroke, pushed the ball to the right side, and knocked it over the second baseman's head, about the same as Chad had done.

Thurlow trotted home with the tying run,

and Chad dug hard for third. But this time the right fielder had played a little shallower. Chad ran as hard as he could, rounded second with his head down, determined to make it to third. But he didn't look up to see that Coach Carlton had his hands in the air, signaling for him to stop at second.

When he heard the coach yell, he hesitated, and that only made things worse. It was too late to turn back, so he dug hard and slid, but the throw was there in plenty of time. He was out.

After all the work the Scrappers had done on this kind of stuff, poor Chad just hadn't been thinking. He got up and, without so much as dusting the dirt off his uniform, ducked his head and ran to the dugout. His father wasn't yelling now. The Pit Bulls were making all the noise.

When Adam struck out, the noise from the Pit Bulls' fans only got louder. They knew they had dodged a bullet. Still, Jeremy was pleased to get the score tied. "All right," he yelled. "Now we got 'em on the run."

Then he walked over to Chad. "Don't worry about getting thrown out. We all mess up some- times. You're the guy who drove in one of the runs we needed. Just think about that."

Chad blew some air out—air that had been stuck in his chest, it seemed. "Thanks, Jeremy," he said. They ran back onto the field together.

CHAPTER TEN

Waxman was coming up first, and the Pit Bulls were pumped up. Adam was tired, but Jeremy thought the coach was right to stay with him. Ollie sometimes took a while to find his motion, and there was no time for that now.

Adam started with a curve, clearly to catch Waxman off stride, but Waxman hit the ball with everything he had. He cracked the ball straight at Tracy. It hit the dirt just in front of her, and she got down for it, but it was coming so wickedly fast that it skipped over her glove, straight into her face.

Tracy spun away from the blow and dropped to the ground. The ball rolled into right field. Jeremy charged in and held Waxman to a single, but Tracy was lying still, and the park was silent.

"Time-out," the umpire finally called, but by then the Scrappers' coaches and players were running toward Tracy. By the time they had collected around her, she was moving. She had dropped her glove and curled up with her hands over her face.

Coach Carlton and Wanda got down on their knees and talked to her. "Let me look at it," Wanda kept saying, but it was some time before Tracy would respond.

When she finally did pull her hands away, Jeremy saw that the ball had scraped her cheekbone, left it red. He knew she was going to have a shiner, but he was afraid the ball might have broken her cheekbone.

"I'm okay," she finally said. "I think I can still play."

"No, not a chance," Coach Carlton said. "We've got to get you to the emergency room over at the medical center and make sure you haven't broken a bone."

Tracy tried to sit up, and when she did, Wanda supported her. "I'm dizzy," Tracy finally admitted.

"Come on," Wanda said. "Some of you kids

give me a hand. I'm going to take her to the hospital."

But by then, Tracy's mom was running onto the field. "I'll take her. How bad is it?" she was asking.

"It's nothing," Tracy said, but she was still hanging on to Wanda. "I want to stay and watch the rest of the game."

"No way," her mother said. "I'm taking you to the hospital to have that looked at."

Jeremy looked at Robbie. "That girl is *tough*," he said.

"*We've* got to get tough," Robbie said. "We need to win this game—more than ever."

Tracy's mom had hold of Tracy now, and the two were headed toward their car. But Mrs. Matlock stopped and looked back. "The Mustangs' game is over. They lost," she told the players. "Now you kids win this game. Okay?"

"We will. I promise," Adam said.

And he walked to the mound. All the players took off for their own positions, and Jeremy felt the determination. But promises were one thing, and winning was another. Everyone was going to have to think and not just play with emotion.

Wayment was up. He looked equally deter-mined to make Adam eat his words—which everyone had heard. But Adam was on fire. He threw two hard strikes at Wayment's knees, and he swung at both of them. Then Adam changed up, and Wayment almost fell down as he swung and missed. Strike three.

Lanman came up looking for fastballs again, and he got a curve. He swung off balance and bumped a little fly to right. Jeremy heard the sound of the ball on the bat and knew that Lan-man hadn't gotten much on it. He took off in-stantly, charging hard. The ball should have dropped in for a single, but Jeremy's reaction, and his speed, got him to the ball. He dived, picked it out of the air, just off the grass. Then he rolled forward into a somersault and popped back to his feet.

Waxman had thought the ball was going to drop. He was halfway to second. Jeremy made the quick and easy throw to first, and Waxman was out. Double play.

The Scrappers went crazy. They charged off the field, everyone screaming and shout-ing. "Now we put them away," Gloria yelled.

"Bottom of the seventh. All we need is a run."

But Coach Carlton grabbed Jeremy as he ran past the third base line. "Wait a second," he said.

Jeremy came to a stop. "Yeah?" He didn't like the way the coach looked—almost upset.

"Tell me the mistake you just made."

"What?"

"You know. Tell me."

Jeremy did know, but he hadn't wanted to think about it. "That was no time to be diving for a ball," he said. "If I had missed it, it would have rolled into right field, and we would have been in a mess."

"That's exactly right. If you stop and take it on one hop, you would have runners on first and second with one out. That's not good, but it's a lot better than letting the go-ahead run score."

"I was sure I could catch it, though."

"Well . . . all right. That's a judgment only a player can make." Suddenly, he grinned—big. "It turned out all right, didn't it?"

"Yes, sir."

"All right. But use your head. Don't get so excited that you do something silly. Okay?"

Jeremy knew what the coach meant. He was

going to be up this inning, and he needed to find a way to get a run. "Okay."

"Jeremy, you still have the green light—unless I take it off. This might be the time to make something happen, but think it through and get the right kind of jump before you go."

Ollie was coming up first, and Jeremy was on deck. What Jeremy hoped was that Ollie would get on, and then Jeremy could think about bunting him over.

As it turned out, Ollie hit a blow that looked like it might end the game. It was to straightaway center and as long a shot as Ollie had ever unloaded. The center fielder ran almost to the fence, but made the catch.

The coach was not pleased. "We need base runners, Jeremy," he yelled. Jeremy knew that was a comment on Ollie's big swing.

Jeremy took a pitch—but the ump called it a strike. Now he would probably have to swing, and the outfielders were all pressing in. No one was looking for a bunt, however, so on the second pitch, Jeremy squared around. He laid down a perfect bunt along the third base line and took off for first.

Then he heard the umpire call, "Foul ball. Strike two."

This couldn't happen. He didn't dare bunt with two strikes, and the element of surprise was gone now anyway.

It was man to man. No walk, no bunt. Jeremy had to stand up to that fastball and do something with it. The next pitch was a blazer, at his chest and a little outside. Jeremy didn't go after it. Ball one.

The next one was closer to the strike zone but still up and away, and now it was 2 and 2.

Gomez was nibbling, not losing control, and Jeremy knew the next pitch was going to be over the plate.

He saw it all the way, got his bat out, and knocked a line drive, low and hard, right up the middle and into center field.

He ran to first, rounded the base, and held. Part of the job was done. The Scrappers were excited, all letting him know he had come through.

Now, somehow, he had to get to second. With one out, a steal made sense, but he knew what the coach had said—only if he could get a good jump. And Gomez would be watching him closely.

He took a strong lead, forced Gomez to throw over. He had to dive back on the throw, but that told him his lead was about right.

On the first pitch, Jeremy bluffed a move to second, and Gomez seemed to hurry his throw. The pitch was high. Jeremy wondered whether he could bother Gomez enough to get a walk for Robbie. Then he wouldn't have to steal.

The idea seemed to work on the next pitch, another ball high, but then Gomez threw a strike.

Jeremy watched the coach. The green light was still on. He had a feeling that Gomez was more worried now about Robbie than he was about keeping Jeremy on first. Jeremy took a shorter lead and then, just as Gomez committed to his windup, took off hard.

The ball was inside, and Robbie had to spin away. Jackson caught the ball and had to step past Robbie to make the throw. But Jeremy had the base stolen. Jackson should have held the ball. Instead, he threw hard—way too hard. As Jeremy slid into second he saw Boone leap in the air, and he saw the ball fly into center field.

Jeremy jumped up immediately, broke toward third, but watched the coach. Coach Carlton was waving for him to come over and then for him to slide. Jeremy made a straight, hard run and then slid into third.

Safe!

This was better than he had hoped: third base with only one out.

The job wasn't finished, however. The game wasn't won. He wanted to do this for Tracy, for the whole team. He wanted to get back into the championship race.

But he had to think.

"Take a lead, be ready," the coach told him.

He walked off the bag and then did a couple of little fake moves, just to distract Gomez. The count was 3 and 1 on Robbie, but a walk didn't mean much here. The Scrappers only needed that one run.

Gomez stepped off the mound. He looked toward the outfield and took a long breath. Then he walked back to the pitching rubber. Jeremy gave him another little head fake, then bounced around a couple of times. He had once seen a major-leaguer steal home, but this was no time to try something like that.

Robbie got ready, and with the pitch, Jeremy broke a few steps down the line. Robbie didn't stroke the ball hard; he merely bounced it toward second base.

"Go!" Coach Carlton yelled. Jeremy was already on his way.

He slid into Jackson as hard as he could, and dust flew, but he knew his left foot was on the plate when the ball smacked into Jackson's glove.

The throw was too late. The Scrappers had won!

Poor Jeremy couldn't get off the ground. Gloria jumped on him first, and then everyone else piled on.

When the craziness was all over and the Scrappers had all slapped hands and shouted until they were hoarse, the coach finally got them to calm down and listen to him. "Kids, you know the Mustangs lost today. That means we're only one game back, but it also means the Mustangs have to lose one more of their final two games, and we have to win both of ours.

They may not lose, and so we may never get our shot at the championship, but here's what I want to say to you."

He waited until everyone was quiet and looking at him. "You started out this season as a bunch of kids with some raw talent and little control. But now you're playing smart, playing together. I hope we can get another shot at the Mustangs, but whether we do or not, just know that you learned to play as a team this year. Don't ever forget what it felt like."

"We better remember it against the Stingrays on Friday," Wilson said.

"Yes. That's exactly right."

Then Cindy said, "Let's go see how Tracy is doing."

The whole team walked down the street to the hospital, which was only a couple of blocks away. They found that Tracy, whose eye was now swollen mostly shut, was badly bruised but had no broken bone.

She grinned—and looked pretty funny—when she found out the team had come through.

The Scrappers learned rather quickly that they weren't welcome around the emergency room. So they all cleared out, and they walked together to Granny's to get some ice cream. Jeremy had a great time, laughing and joking and talking about the big win. Afterward, he walked back to the park with Robbie to get their bikes. "That was smart the way you bounced that ball, nice and slow, to the right side," Jeremy told him.

"Hey, I knew you'd score. You're fast, and you know how to run the bases."

Jeremy liked that. And he liked hanging out with Robbie. Now he just hoped that, somehow, the Scrappers might get a shot at the championship.

TIPS FOR PLAYING CENTER FIELD

1. A center fielder needs good wheels and a great arm—speed *and* power. This is the position played by Mickey Mantle, Willie Mays and Joe DiMaggio—players who could do it all.
2. The center fielder takes control in the outfield. You have to be ready to cover a lot of ground, but you also have to make decisions and be in charge. If you can get to a ball, you take it yourself and call off the left or right fielder.
3. Great major league center fielders play fairly shallow to cut off ground balls before they turn into doubles. But that means they have to be able to go back fast and make catches with their backs to home plate. Don't expect to do that in the beginning, but practice that catch until you can make it.
4. A center fielder has to get a great "jump" on the ball. So stay on the balls of your feet as the pitcher gets ready to throw. You may not see any action for an inning or two, but when the ball does come your way, you have to make a quick judgment and break to the ball—so don't be daydreaming.
5. Watch the ball as it comes off the bat and listen to the sound it makes so you'll know how well it's hit. Learn to judge how far a ball will travel and where it will end up. Don't be lazy about getting to that spot as quickly as you can.
6. On a high fly ball, don't stand under it, but stay a step or two back. Then come toward the infield as you catch the ball, take a little hop for power

and balance, and know by then where you're going to throw.

7. Outfielders rarely throw all the way home. When you catch a ball, or field a grounder in the outfield, throw a dart at your cutoff's head. Let the cutoff player decide whether the ball should go on through. On a ball hit in front of you, charge hard—then a play at home might be possible.

8. When the action is in the infield, don't assume you have nothing to do. Back up second base on any throw, whether from the catcher or an infielder. Charge toward second as though you are convinced the infielder will *not* make the catch. Most of the time, you won't have to help, but when you do, you just might cut off a run from scoring.

9. When the ball is hit to left or right field, is that a good time for you to watch and rest? No, of course not! Center fielders run! Get over there and back up your teammate.

10. No matter how fast you are, you need to be in the right defensive position. That means you have to know the hitters in your league, and know your pitcher. If you shift a step to your right, and that makes the difference on getting to a ball hit in the gap, you've saved the day with your head, not just your feet and your glove.

SOME RULES FROM COACH CARLTON

HITTING:

Don't make it easy on the pitcher by swinging at bad pitches. Your chances of getting a hit go way down when you swing at pitches out of the strike zone.

BASE RUNNING:

If you're on base and a fly ball is hit to the outfield, your coach may tell you to "play it halfway." Run halfway to the next base and then watch what happens. If the outfielder makes the catch, hurry back to the base you were on. If the outfielder can't make the catch, go hard for the next base or beyond.

BEING A TEAM PLAYER:

Baseball is a *great* game. Respect the game and respect everyone who plays it. If your teammates do something well, let them know it. And don't be afraid to tell players on another team that they've done a good job.

ON DECK:
TRACY MATLOCK, SECOND BASE.
DON'T MISS HER STORY IN SCRAPPERS #8: *NO FEAR.*

Ollie got the first pitch outside, but way outside, and Badger didn't swing. The next pitch was close, and Badger took a cut and missed.

Now Wilson moved the target to the inside edge, and Ollie tried to bust him in tight. The pitch was close, barely inside, but Badger spun away and shouted to the umpire, "He's throwing at me again."

Tracy heard the umpire say, "That pitch was almost in the strike zone."

Badger seemed to know better than to complain much more. He stepped back to the plate. This time Ollie went back outside, and Badger took another big swing—and connected. He sent a hard shot on the ground, straight at Tracy.

Tracy had only a moment to react. She stayed low and got her glove down, but the ball skipped high and bounced off the heel of her glove. She had stayed in front of the ball, and it dropped on the ground where she could grab it. She picked it up and made an easy throw to Adam for the out.

It was actually a routine play. She had done everything right. Almost everything.

All the Scrappers were yelling, "Way to go, Trace. Good job." But Tracy looked over at Gloria, and Gloria looked troubled. Tracy immediately looked away. She socked her fist into her glove and walked back to her position. She didn't want to admit it to herself, but she knew the truth. At the last instant, as the ball had come up on her, she had looked away, turned her head to avoid taking another blow in the face.

Maybe she wouldn't have fielded the ball cleanly anyway. But she knew she hadn't looked the ball into her glove. Had she been afraid? Was she going to be afraid from now on?

Jefferson was up. She needed to think about that. He was very slow, so she could cheat back just a little. It gave her more time to field a ground ball and still throw him out. He could hit the ball hard, and it helped to have a little more room to work. Or was she moving back because she was scared?

"Hit it right here, Jefferson," Tracy chanted. "I got your number."

But she knew she was just trying to convince herself of that. She was hoping he would hit it somewhere else, that she wouldn't have to handle another tough play right now.

As it turned out, Jefferson didn't hit the ball anywhere. Ollie kept him off balance. He pitched the ball in and out, changed speeds, and finally struck Jefferson out on a mean fastball at the knees and on the outer edge.

So the Scrappers still had their lead, and Tracy was going to get a chance to make something happen on offense. As she ran off the field, she shouted, "All right. Let's get some runs now."

But she didn't look at Gloria. She ran to the bat rack and found the bat she always used. She walked away from the other players and took some swings. She was going to handle ol' Bullet this time.

But as she walked to the plate, she felt the butterflies in her stomach—worse than she remembered in a long time. Was it because her friends from her neighborhood were there? Or was it because the game meant so much?

Or was it Bennett's fastball?

She purposefully set up a little closer to the plate than usual. She wanted Bennett to see that she was right there, ready to go after him.

But when Bennett released his first pitch, she saw the ball boring through the air straight at her head. She dropped on the ground to get out of the way.

As she was falling, she knew that the pitch hadn't been that close after all.

"Ball one!" the umpire said. At least it hadn't been a strike.

Badger was laughing again. He didn't say a word, but she knew what he was thinking—that she was afraid of Bennett.

She dug in again and this time set herself. If he hit her in the forehead, she wasn't going to back away. But this pitch was over the plate, and Tracy didn't trigger. She felt frozen in her stance, and she didn't know why.

She couldn't do that again. But the next pitch was low, and she went after it anyway. She fouled it into the dirt.

"Come on, Tracy. Concentrate," the coach was yelling. "Stroke this one."

But Bennett threw another inside pitch.

At least Tracy didn't hit the dirt. She took a hard swing. But she felt herself stepping away as she swung. She missed the ball and struck out.

And Badger was still laughing.

"Shut up," Tracy told him as she walked away. And then she took off her batting helmet and tossed it toward the bat rack. When she walked into the dugout, she sat down at the closest end, so she wouldn't have to walk past everyone.

Gloria got up, came over to her, and sat down. "What's going on?" she asked.

"Nothing."

"Don't give me that. You're acting like little Miss Prissy out there."

"Shut up."

"You took a dive, and the ball was almost over the plate. You're thinking more about your cute little face than you are about our game."

"Shut up, Gloria. You don't know what it's like." The words came out before she had had time to think. She had admitted more than she wanted to.

"What are you talking about? You think I've never been hit by a ground ball?"

"Not like I got hit."

"Oh, come on. That's stuff your mom is feeding you." Gloria changed her voice to a high-pitched, simpering tone. "You won't ever be prom queen, my little sweety, if you get bumps all over your face."

"Just shut up. I can handle anything you can."

"Well, then, prove it." Gloria got up and walked back to where she had been sitting before, next to Thurlow and Wilson.

Tracy was furious. She vowed to herself that she wouldn't mess up again. But Gloria was wrong about one thing. Tracy wasn't afraid of getting another black eye just because it would look bad. She was simply scared of the ball. She had been telling herself all the right things, but she couldn't seem to control her reaction, and that reaction was to protect herself from getting hit in the face again.